Cécile GATES of GOLD

GIRLS *of* MANY LANDS

England ✈ 1592
Isabel: Taking Wing by Annie Dalton

France ✈ 1711
Cécile: Gates of Gold by Mary Casanova

China ✈ 1857
Spring Pearl: The Last Flower by Laurence Yep

Yup'ik Alaska ✈ 1890
Minuk: Ashes in the Pathway by Kirkpatrick Hill

India ✈ 1939
Neela: Victory Song by Chitra Banerjee Divakaruni

Cécile GATES of GOLD

by Mary Casanova

American Girl

Visit our Web site at **americangirl.com**

Printed in China.
02 03 04 05 06 07 C&C 10 9 8 7 6 5 4 3 2 1

Girls of Many Lands™, Cécile™, and American Girl®
are trademarks of Pleasant Company.

PERMISSIONS & PICTURE CREDITS

The following individuals and organizations have generously given
permission to reprint illustrations contained in "Then and Now":
p. 181—Réunion des Musées Nationaux/Art Resource, NY
(*View of the Chateau de Versailles*, by Pierre Patel, 1668);
pp. 182–183—Musée de la Marine/49.OA.1 (mask); reproduced
by permission of the Trustees of the Wallace Collection, London
(*Madame de Ventadour with portraits of Louis XIV and his heirs*, French
School, c. 1715–20, by Nicolas de Largillière);
Réunion des Musées Nationaux/Art Resource, NY (*View of the
Chateau de Versailles*, by Pierre Patel, 1668);
pp. 184–185—Los Angeles County Museum of Art, Costume Council
Fund (stays); Victoria & Albert Picture Library,
London (shoe); pp. 186–187—Réunion des Musées Nationaux/Art
Resource, NY (*Peasant Family*, by Louis Le Nain);
© Catherine Karnow/CORBIS (French schoolgirls);
© Robert Holmes/CORBIS (Versailles today).

Illustration by Jean-Paul Tibbles

**Cataloging-in-Publication Data available from
the Library of Congress**

For my daughter, Kate Elise

*And a grateful acknowledgment to Cindy Rogers,
for joining me on a research trip to Versailles;
Tamara England, for offering editorial insight and
encouragement; Sally Wood, for assisting with
historical research; my writers' groups, for listening
and responding; and my family, for being there
every step of the journey.*

Contents

1 Runaway Horse

I was alone in the forest near Rileaux, my village,
when the earth trembled beneath my feet. As I
dropped to the forest floor my basket toppled,
scattering my carefully gathered mushrooms
everywhere. Flattened against the ground, I crept
beneath a fringe of cedar and studied the sunlit
meadow beyond. Wildflowers bent to a light breeze.
Bees lifted from clover to clover as thundering
hoofbeats pulsed steadily closer.

I recalled my father's reminder. "Be careful,
Cécile," he'd warned when I'd set out that noon.
"Times being what they are, you can't trust strangers
or soldiers."

I had heard many stories about King Louis XIV's
soldiers and how they fed off villages, leaving the

villages more barren of food, if that was possible, than when the soldiers arrived. My father and I had enough trouble putting food on our table. The mushrooms were for our soup, and I wouldn't give them up without a fight—after I gathered them again, that was.

Pressed to the damp ground, I kept watch and waited, wary as a stray. In my village, homeless dogs that stayed at arm's length managed to survive. Those that too easily became pets sometimes ended up in the cook pot of a peasant who had suffered a poor harvest.

In the meadow, packs of baying hounds ran by, noses to the ground. My skin prickled. What if they caught my scent? But luckily, I was downwind, and they were intent on tracking a scent the length of the meadow. Soon after the dogs went by, a legion of horses galloped past, carrying riders dressed in gold, silver, and velvet and wearing plumed hats. In the throng, four ponies pulled a gilded cart in which a dark-wigged man sat tall, his gaze fixed on the chase. A few of the riders were dressed completely in black, and even the riders who were brightly adorned wore a hint of black—a scarf, a cape, or a ribbon—signs of mourning, I guessed, for the *dauphin*, the king's son, who had died a few months earlier.

"The stag headed through here!" someone shouted.

"Straight on, dogs!" another yelled.

"For the glory of France! For the glory of the Sun King!"

Bugles sounded, cheering followed, and as quickly as the hunting party had appeared, it faded away, the earth rumbling softly at its departure.

I drew a breath. The king's hunting party! Who else but the king had such a wealth of beautiful dogs and horses . . . such finery? The elderly man in the cart had likely been King Louis XIV, who was in his seventies and who still loved hunting. He must have been on a hunt from his nearest estate, Marly, where he was said to go to escape the court life at the palace of Versailles. The Sun King himself. I trembled. If I lived at Versailles, if I were a duchess or princess, or even a servant of the court, I knew in my teeth that life would be heaven.

But my life was anything but royal. Practically every day was a struggle to make do. And two years past, when I was ten, if there had been more food on our table and wood for our fire, *Maman* might have survived the bitter cold and her pneumonia. Many people froze in their beds that winter—the winter of 1709. Olive groves and grain froze. Goats, sheep, cows, and chickens froze. Rabbits froze in their dens. Even the king's table wine froze at Versailles. And following the severe cold came famine.

At least I had my mother's clothes. But her once beautiful embroidered blouse was now dirt-gray, her long skirt stitched and restitched, hemmed and patched every year to fit my tiny yet growing frame. I was sick of wearing the same dingy clothes month after month. My father didn't notice. If he would at least charge every patient who came to see him, we might not be so terribly poor. Even an ox was smart enough to expect hay in return for its work. But my kindhearted father treated anyone who came to him, whether they could pay or not.

If I lived at court, I would wear a new gown, all my own. No, I would have many gowns, a different one for every day of the year, and each of a rich fabric and color. Every day, I would ride in a gilded coach. Every evening, I would charm my suitors at an over-flowing banquet table and, after eating my fill, I would dance by the light of a thousand candles.

I rose to my feet, brushed flecks of moss and earth from my skirt, then curtsied and bowed my head to an imaginary courtier. As I did, my head scarf fell forward and my hair dropped around my face.

Short blasts of air and a loud snort startled me. I spun around, flinging my hair back from my eyes, and braced myself against the intruder.

A few steps away, an ebony horse pranced in an arc around my abandoned basket, then stopped, eyeing it as if it were a coiled snake. His nostrils flared with each breath and his eyes were opened wide as shutters. Sweat lathered his muscular neck, chest, and flanks. His bridle was trimmed in royal blue and gold, and his leather reins hung loose. On his back sat an elaborately carved wooden saddle.

"*Non, non*, sweet horse," I said. "Please don't trample my mushrooms." I used the same soothing voice my father used with frightened children whose broken arms or legs he was asked to mend. "Now, boy," I continued, gently but confidently. If I showed fear, the horse would know it and run. He pawed at the ground, then tossed his head up, as far as his breast strap would allow.

I had to catch him and return him to his rightful owner. But if I stepped toward him, I feared he would bolt. So instead I deliberately turned my back to him, as if to act uninterested. I had made friends with many stray dogs this way, though, of course, I never ate them. I waited, my hands behind my back, pretending to enjoy the view of the meadow more than anything in the world. Whose horse was this? And where was his fallen rider? I scanned the meadow but saw no one.

A warm nudge at my hand told me I had succeeded. "See, you didn't really want to run away, did you? Your duty is to serve your master." Slowly, I turned. The wildness in the horse's dark eyes had faded. I gently grasped his reins and rubbed his damp neck. "Now, what shall I do with you?"

The vision of a reward, a small but bulging velvet bag of coins, filled my mind. I saw myself kneeling at the king's throne, but before I could accept the outstretched pouch, I was startled back to reality.

A woman's voice, faint and pained, sounded from the shadows. "*Au secours!*" The words were French, but the accent was not. "*S'il vous plaît!*" she called. "Help! Please, help!"

2 An Unexpected Reward

I listened hard but heard nothing. Beneath cedar, pine, and scrub oak, a carpet of ferns and moss covered the forest floor, muffling sounds. A swallow darted over my head, then broke from the shadows into the meadow.

"*Bonjour?*" I called. "Hello? Where are you?"

The woman moaned in reply.

I followed the direction of her voice, and led the horse down a tangled slope of roots and logs to the base of a muddy ravine. There, in a rumpled mass of lavender skirts and a velvet riding jacket, lay a stout woman. The fabric at her left shoulder was ripped, and her shoulder protruded awkwardly. I had seen this condition before. The woman moaned between gritted teeth. Her plumed hat lay in mud beside a log,

and beneath her white hair, her pockmarked face
was contorted with pain. I guessed her to be the age
of a grandmother and was amazed she was fit enough
to ride with the hunting party.

"You need help," I said.

For an instant, the woman opened her eyes of
piercing blue, then closed them again. Tears
squeezed from the edges of her lashes.

I wished that I had the strength of a man to hoist
the woman up and onto the horse's back. Instead, all
I could do was to listen for the sound of approaching
horses and hope that a search was under way. Other
than the song of a nightingale, the forest was silent.

"*Madame*," I said soothingly. "My father, he helps
many, many people who come to him. I can't help

you, but perhaps he can." The horse lowered his head to a patch of grass. I debated riding him home to get my father, but I didn't want to get caught with a royal horse—I didn't need to be accused of stealing, which brought a penalty of flogging, or even death. Instead, I tied the horse to the nearest tree.

"I'll return as quickly as possible," I said. The woman barely nodded in return.

As fast as I could run, I retraced my path through the forest. Before long, struggling to catch my breath, I was at our thatched hut on the edge of Rileaux. I burst through the door to find my father beside the window, studying an open book as he arranged various bones on our eating board. In a rush of words, I told him about catching the horse and finding the noblewoman.

"*Oui*," he said, between deep coughs that forced him to hunch forward. "Yes, we must do what we can." He turned to our wooden bucket and washed his hands.

"Papa," I said impatiently, "the woman doesn't care what you look like."

My father scolded me by raising his eyebrows. He didn't rule our home like so many fathers did, with yelling and beatings. One village woman had told him I was spoiled because I spoke my mind with him, but in truth, he was the one who had encouraged me to do so.

"It is better for her health," he said, "if my hands are clean." Then he gathered his leather case of instruments and followed me out the door and into the forest.

When I came upon my overturned basket, I said, "This way, Papa." He caught up with me moments later at the edge of the ravine. Without a word, he hobbled down to the woman, who was hunched into a ball of pain and breathing shallowly. As my father knelt beside her, the woman glanced up at him. A look of surprise—or perhaps of relief—passed over her eyes, and then she closed them again.

My father ran his hands gently over her shoulder and arm. The woman cried out. He lifted her chin and studied her neck. Many people called my father a crazy peasant, but never those who went away feeling better after his care.

"Stay still and try to relax, Madame," he told the woman as I stood aside, stroking the horse's neck. He looked at me. "Cécile, I need your help."

At his instruction, I helped him roll the woman onto her back as she shrieked at us in a foreign language. Droplets of sweat formed on her forehead, and her teeth chattered.

"This will hurt for a moment," he said, "and then you will feel much better."

I kneeled by the woman's head and, with both hands, put my weight on her shoulders to hold her down. With experienced hands, my father gripped her elbow and pulled down forcefully. The woman cried out, and her shoulder made a slight popping sound.

My father glanced at me with a nod, and I sat back on my heels and waited, as I had done before, with other patients.

For many moments, the woman lay back, as if dead. Gradually, her breathing returned to normal and the pain washed from her face. She wiped her forehead with the back of her gloved hand.

"*Mon Dieu!*" she said, opening her eyes.

She clenched and unclenched her right hand, touched her shoulder, and after a few moments, struggled to sit. I gave her my hand. Finally, with our help, she stood, towering over us, one hand to her shoulder.

"It's still sore . . . but . . . truly, you worked a miracle," she said.

My father nodded in response. "You will feel sore for some time, but a little ice—which I hear you can obtain even in summer at Versailles—will help it heal more quickly."

I wondered how my father knew she was from the Sun King's court. But of course, no one in our village dressed as fine as this woman did, so it was a natural conclusion. Certainly, she would offer to pay my father or to reward him in some way. If ever there was an opportunity to better our lives, the moment was upon us. I held my breath.

"*Merci beaucoup, Monsieur,*" she said, with her slight accent. "Thank you!"

My father answered with a low bow, sweeping his hand with grace to the ground. I had never seen him use such manners.

The woman straightened her skirt and untied her horse from the tree. "Spooked by a tiny rabbit," she said. "Taking me on a wild ride through the trees. Shame on you!" She patted the horse's shoulder, adjusted his saddle, and then turned to me.

"Thank you, also, *Mademoiselle*."

I bowed my head, curtsied, and stumbled on my words. "Your Gracious Highness—I mean, Queen."

"You're close," she said in her accented way. "I am neither the queen, who is dead, nor the king's 'secret' wife, Madame de Maintenon, whom everyone knows about, and so that's hardly a secret in all of France. I am Elisabeth Charlotte of Germany, *la Duchesse d'Orléans*, sister-in-law to the king, and known by most everyone simply as 'Madame.'"

"Madame," I said again with a curtsy.

"I see you are not without manners. What's your name, and by what courage did you come to catch my skittish, ill-behaved horse?"

"My name is Cécile Revel, Madame." I swallowed past the sudden dryness in my throat. "My father has taught me to observe closely. I have learned a few things about calming animals, that is all. I am far from courageous. Quite the opposite, in fact."

"Revel, is it?" She glanced from me to my father, studying him. My father met her eyes and nodded. Madame continued, her eyes fixed upon my father's face. "I see. How can I repay you, my dear Monsieur Revel, for your kindness and skill, and for that of your daughter as well?"

At last! This once, I hoped my father would demand a large sum of money. Please, God above, a purse of money. For a season, we would have food on our table, and I would buy fabric for a new skirt and perhaps buy a pair of soft leather shoes to replace my wooden clogs. I shifted my glance away from the woman to my father, whose eyes were downcast, a sign that he was deep in thought. I waited.

Finally, he looked up, his eyebrows twitching. "Just one request, Madame," he said, starting to cough again from deep in his chest. "That my

daughter, whom I love above life itself, be spared
a peasant's future . . . and be granted a position
at court."

I couldn't believe what I had heard. I had
dreamed of life at court, but now that his request
was made, my heart fluttered. Dizziness overcame
me and I feared I might faint, yet I stood strong.

"Can you read?" Madame asked.

I nodded.

"Quite well," my father added.

"And you appear to be good with animals, is this
true?"

"Oh yes," my father said. "She is, indeed."
He took the horse's reins, extended his hand to
Madame, and helped her up to a nearby log and
into her saddle.

"Very well, Monsieur," Madame said, settling
herself sidesaddle with a groan. She turned to me.
"Cécile, I have six little dogs in need of a new servant to help care for them. My former girl recently
married and moved to Paris. With your calming
ways, you may be just right for the position. You and

your father have helped me and, in return, I will grant his request."

I could not form any words, not even one. Many girls my age began lives in the convent or were soon married off. The likelihood of marrying a peasant loomed closer every year. Now, here was the chance to serve at court. I should be delighted. Instead, I was numb.

I glanced at my father, whose eyes were brimming. I couldn't bear the thought of leaving him alone. His cough was growing worse with every week, and he needed me. Yet his request for me was a position at court, and though my mind swam with protest, I knew I had no choice in the matter. Girls my age did not decide their own futures. My duty was clear.

"Merci, Madame," I whispered, barely able to speak. "Thank you."

3 A Warning

After trailing for hours beside Madame's horse through meadow and forest and meadow again, all the way to the king's hunting estate of Marly, my feet were swollen and blistered from walking so far in my wooden *sabots*. I was used to walking everywhere, but not over such a distance, for I never had traveled much beyond my village. But my feet were the last thing on my mind as a dozen soldiers rode out to meet us. They discovered it was Madame and rode back to alert the king that we were on our way.

As I walked beside Madame into the courtyard of Marly, my heart pattered like a caged mouse. The sun was low as Madame's horse clattered over cobblestones. If this was a hunting estate, with fountains, waterfalls, and flower beds—with

buildings larger than our village church—I could not begin to imagine the palace at Versailles.

At a large square stone, Madame dismounted, and a groom took the horse's reins. The king, the man I had seen in the cart, stepped out to greet us, followed by at least fifty courtiers. He was tall, with a rounded belly and somber expression beneath a curled, shoulder-length brown wig. Though he walked with a cane, his pace was amazingly brisk as he strode to Madame's side.

"A search party was sent for you," he said, "but I see you delivered yourself back to us."

A slight flush rose to Madame's face. "With some help, Your Grace," Madame said, with a nod to me.

"Tell us," the king said, with a beckoning sweep of

his hand to the crowd behind him.

Despite her mud-caked garments, Madame stood tall and told about her fall, her rescue, and how she had decided to take me into her service. As soon as she finished, the king announced, "A splendid story! Now, let us celebrate Madame's well-being by returning to the gaming tables, with huge winnings for some and losses for others!"

Applause followed. Then Madame, without so much as a good-bye to me, walked arm-in-arm with the king into the building. My feet were planted on the cobblestones. I had no idea what I was to do next. As the crowd thinned, a young woman tapped me on the shoulder.

"Follow me," she said, her chestnut hair styled high above her ivory forehead. She smelled of lavender. "I am Françoise, Madame's lady-in-waiting. She asked me to see to you."

I curtsied, ashamed at my filthy clothes. Head high, Françoise led me through a maze of corridors and rooms of such wealth—marble statues, wall-sized paintings and mirrors, tapestry carpets—that I could hardly breathe. Soon, in a smaller room of white tiles, several waiting women tended to me. They commanded me to remove my clothes and climb into a tub of steaming water, something I had never done before. In the hot water, my skin turned as pink as wild roses. "An occasional bath is helpful," one of the women said as she lathered my hair.

"Yes, especially when a body is so dirty one can hardly tell if it's a boy or girl beneath the grime."

"But too much water," another said, "will certainly bring ill health. A little rubbing of cloth against skin, that's enough to—"

An elderly woman dressed in black stepped into the bathing room. The maids stopped talking and parted like the Red Sea for Moses. Over the woman's thin shoulders was draped a black lace shawl, and over the shawl hung a gold cross, studded with jewels that shimmered in the candlelight. She stood over my tub, and wrinkles deepened into a crevice between her eyes.

"And you are Madame's new servant?" she asked, disgust pulling at the edges of her pale lips.

I nodded and lowered my gaze. "Oui, Madame."

"Madame de Maintenon," she said. "Not to be confused with 'Madame,' who does nothing but complain and stir up trouble. She tells me you come from noble blood and that you deserve a position at court. Does she think I'm a fool to fall for such a lie?"

I kept my lips sealed. Certainly Madame was stretching the truth about noble blood. Perhaps she had to lie to honor my father's request.

"Your every move will be watched, Mademoiselle. Remember that, lest you are here on a mission to spy or to poison the king."

"Poison? No!" I nearly jumped from the bath. How could she imply such a thing? "I would never think—"

"Enough," she said, her palm up, stopping my protest. "It's a warning. At court, we can never be too careful."

Then, as quietly as she had entered the room, she was gone.

The maids let out a collective sigh and began to whisper among themselves. As soon as I was scrubbed from scalp to toenails, one woman pulled a white gown over my head, another combed my hair brusquely, and yet another showed me to a small bed for the night. I didn't believe I would sleep, but I did.

At dawn, a gentle voice awakened me. "Put this on," said Françoise, holding out a gown of dusty green with a tiny waist and tufted sleeves. A light *chemise* hung over her arm.

"But," I said, "I'm supposed to help with Madame's dogs. That cannot be for me."

"It was made last night," Françoise said. "Sewn especially for you."

I couldn't imagine that, as servant of the dogs, so much money would be spent on me. Village children ran around half-naked for lack of clothes.

"The king demands an elegant court. The gates of Versailles are open to all who wish to enter, as long as they are dressed properly. Hurry, we leave for the palace shortly."

With Françoise's help, I slipped into the soft
chemise and then into the gown. Someone must
have measured me while I slept, for the clothes fit
perfectly. Next, I put on a pair of stockings and
shoes that matched my dress. The felt shoes were a
little tight on my swollen feet, but I was not about to
complain. Finally, Françoise stuck a bit of bread in
my hand as she brushed my hair.

"Now eat," she said. "And fast."

My dream had indeed come true. I longed to
show my maman, now gone, how I looked—and
my father, who had requested such a future for me.
Then I remembered Madame de Maintenon's
warning, which fell like a shadow across my dream.

"The king's coaches are ready and waiting!" came
a voice from the distance. Trumpets sounded. With
a rustle of linen and silk, I set off after Françoise
down the halls. Voices grew in volume, and soon
I was back in the courtyard amid courtiers and
servants, and near Madame herself, whose back was
turned to me. I tried to breathe, but I could barely
manage in the tight waist of my new dress and at the

sight of so much finery. As if in a dream, I watched it all with a strange sense of distance.

The king, in a teal cape trimmed in white ermine, his head high and face expressionless, strode to the largest carriage. Behind him walked Madame de Maintenon, chin high and shoulders stiff, garbed in black from her lace shawl to her trailing dress.

After her, a young woman and man, both elegantly dressed and with rich locks of brown, stepped lightly forward, arm in arm, as if they were about to dance together. They glanced at one another and smiled. At the woman's side skipped a singing young boy of about five, with sandy, shoulder-length curls. He suddenly stopped singing and skipped back to what appeared to be his governess, for the elderly woman gave him a stern look and a soft snap of her fingers. The boy walked dutifully beside her. Another woman carried a toddler, whose clothing was of the same red as the man and woman's ahead.

"That," whispered Françoise, "is the beloved princess—Marie-Adélaïde—and her husband, the prince—*le Duc de Bourgogne*—and their children, who are the great-grandchildren of the king."

At that moment, I fell in love with the young royal family. They were the fairy-tale family I had wished for: a father and mother who cared for one another— as my parents had—and their happy children. The sight of them filled me with pleasure and a sense of hope mixed with a deep sadness, somewhat like the bitter chocolate I had once tasted at our village fair. Yesterday, there had been no time to return to my village or to say a proper good-bye to my father. He had walked with us to the edge of the meadow, kissed me on each cheek, and whispered in my ear, "You are my pride, Cécile. Be true to who you are." I promised I would write to him, and then I headed off with Madame, looking over my shoulder as I walked empty-handed across the field. My father stood motionless, watching us leave, as we crested the nearest slope and disappeared. As I remembered that moment, my throat tightened with emotion, and I clenched my teeth. This was not the place to cry.

Madame stepped forward from the crowd. Knowing that I was in her service, I took a step in her direction, but was stopped short. Françoise held me by my elbow. "Wait!" she whispered in my ear. "The first thing to learn, Cécile, is that every single event, every single movement at court, comes with a set of rules. It's called *etiquette*. Many a position has been lost for not knowing who goes first."

I nodded, only slightly, hoping no one else had seen my mistake. I had no knowledge of the rules. How was I to know if I was breaking a rule if I had never been taught it? My stomach tensed with foreboding. My position at court might be as delicate as handling a raw egg in its shell.

I waited silently for Françoise's directions.

To my surprise, a footman soon approached us. "Your presence is requested by la Duchesse d'Orléans, Elisabeth Charlotte."

I wasn't sure what he was talking about. Then it hit me. *Oh, he meant Madame!*

Several women turned their heads toward me, their hair piled high, looks of surprise on their white-painted, sleepy faces. They whispered among themselves.

"Walk slowly," Françoise whispered in my ear, "and stay right behind me."

And I did so. At long last, I reached the coach, hoped I would not stumble as I climbed up, and found myself within.

"Very good, Cécile," Madame said with a slight nod of approval. "You carry yourself with a natural grace, and I shouldn't wonder."

With my feet pinched and sore in my new shoes, I marveled that I hadn't stumbled to the ground in front of everyone. I wanted to ask what she meant—"I shouldn't wonder"—but after Françoise's warning about rules and etiquette, and Madame de Maintenon's strange visit the night before, I decided my question could wait. Already my imagined tapestry of life at court was beginning to fray.

"You look overwhelmed by all this, child. And yet, Marly is much smaller than Versailles," Madame said, as our coach started off with a jolt. "Sometimes I get lost in the vastness of the palace, which is why I love my dogs so much. They give me companionship in what can be one of the loneliest places on earth."

4 The Palace

Never had I imagined that a ride in a gilded coach, carved with dolphins and cherubs and lined in blue velvet, could be as bumpy as a ride in a hay wagon. I was nearly jostled off my cushioned seat across from Madame not once, but countless times.

"How are your feet this morning?" she asked.

"Much better, thank you," I lied.

"With me," Madame said, "I want you to speak the truth, no matter what. Do I need to ask again?"

I hesitated. "My feet are swollen this morning, Madame. My shoes, though quite lovely, are a bit tight."

"We've a long ride ahead of us. Take off your shoes and put up your feet. No one will see you but Françoise and me."

I did so, then turned to watch the scenery float by through the coach's glass window. Whenever the road turned or twisted, I marveled at the dozens of other carriages in the king's procession.

By midmorning, storm clouds gathered like dark wolves behind us. Seated beside Françoise, I was facing backward and I watched the angry sky. Lightning shivered through muddy clouds, thunder echoed off the hills, and the wind howled down upon us, fairly lifting our coach off the road.

I had never learned to be calm in the midst of a storm. "Madame," I asked, "will the driver stop and find shelter?"

"Not likely," she said, her hands folded in her lap. "The king wants to be back in time for his council meeting. When he makes up his mind, nothing gets in his way."

The coach jolted forward, and our driver whipped the team of eight horses into a gallop. "Hang on," Madame said, grabbing velvet handles on the inside walls of the coach. Françoise and I did the same.

We bumped and jostled as the coach doubled its

speed. Rain overtook us and pelted the windows. "Will we tip over?" I asked, hand clenched white on the handle.

"Perhaps," Madame said. "It's happened before. But God takes our lives when it's time, not a second before. So why worry? Did you know, Cécile, that yesterday's fall was my twenty-fifth in all my years of hunting?"

I shook my head.

"And yet," she said with a smile, "here I am. Thanks, in part, to your help, of course."

I nodded, wishing I possessed half of Madame's courage and certainty.

We traveled on, keeping pace with the storm. Our coach swayed and tilted with the force of the wind. Puddles splashed in great sheets as the coach sped along the increasingly muddy road.

And then, as we skirted another village, a jolt sent me flying into Madame's lap when our coach stopped abruptly. I clamored back to my seat, heat rising to my face. "Forgive me, Madame," I said, ashamed of myself. I owed it to my father not to fail in my new position.

Unfazed, Madame gazed ahead out her window. Muffled shouts and screams came from the front of our procession. After a few moments of waiting, she tapped on the roof of the coach. The driver opened the door, his jacket and face dotted with mud. "Oui, Madame?"

"Is the king safe? What's going on up ahead?"

"Peasants were in the way of the king's coach," he said.

"And?"

"They were trampled," he said. He looked ahead, shielding his eyes from the driving rain.

"Oh, how awful," Madame said. "Go closer. Give me a full report."

Within moments, the driver returned. "Children, Madame. Two children playing in the mud. If their parents had been watching them—" He stopped. "The king is giving coins to the families. We will be under way soon, Madame."

"Merci," she said.

The door closed again, protecting us from the rain

and enclosing us, dry and warm, in Madame's velvet-lined carriage. I remembered the bag of coins I had so earnestly desired, but at what price? If one of the children had been a friend or sister or brother, no amount of coins would have mattered. I sat quietly, hoping my face didn't reveal my feelings.

All too soon, the coaches started off and passed a crowd of peasants huddled by two small bodies on the edge of the muddy road. The image haunted me. I couldn't believe that our driver had blamed the parents. Peasants had no governesses or ladies-in-waiting to help them with their needs. The children's parents were probably both working in the fields to keep their children from starving—and to pay their share of the king's taxes. Was the king so busy that the coaches couldn't have stopped for two children? Were the lives of his subjects of so little worth—a few coins?

We continued at the same heart-rattling speed. Within the hour, the storm had passed, but my dark thoughts lingered. Beneath the brilliant sun, steam rose from the wet ground. Fields and vineyards gave way to rows of manicured trees, shops, and guilds.

Our coach rounded a corner where a bony woman stood with a child huddled in her skirts. "Bread!" she shrieked, her fist raised as we passed. "We have no bread!"

"A shortage of food and money," Madame said, shaking her head. "Everywhere, it is the same. Hunger makes people crazy, like that poor woman. But what can be done?"

I wondered how many loaves of bread Madame's gold brooch, set with shining jewels, might buy.

The coach traveled on, and the dirt road changed to cobblestone. The day was turning hot, and strands of my hair, dampened with sweat, stuck to my neck and forehead.

Our coaches paused at a building, its courtyard a huge semicircle bustling with ornate coaches and glistening horses that were saddled and ready to ride. Soldiers in blue and gold uniforms, marking them as the king's, stood in formation.

"Is that the palace?" I asked, gesturing out my window.

Françoise laughed. "No, that is one of two such stables." She pointed out her window. "That is the palace."

I turned and stared.

The palace was larger than any cathedral, wider than any peasant's field, and an expanse of cobblestone led up a slope to its golden gates. Beyond the gates, sunlight glinted from a thousand windows, and like a small heavenly city, the stone buildings of Versailles rose as if to the clouds.

Trumpets sounded, and soldiers started marching in front of the royal caravan as we lurched forward. "The king," Madame said, fanning herself, "always returns with a celebration. Like the sun itself, life at court is marked by when the king rises in the morning and when he goes to bed at night."

Our coach followed in procession through the golden gates. Music like nothing I had ever heard before filled the courtyard. When Françoise and I finally stepped out of the coach—long after Madame, who had been carried off in an enclosed sedan chair by four footmen—I spotted dozens and dozens of musicians playing stringed instruments. I had heard three or four minstrels play, but never so many musicians at once.

I waited by Françoise's side in a growing crowd of thousands. Never had I seen so many people before, and I worried I would be crushed by the crowd. Françoise noticed my worry and explained that as many as ten thousand people lived and worked at the palace. She said that to earn the ear of the king or a position at court was a life goal for nobility, foreigners, and merchants.

The music swelled, and the king, Madame de Maintenon, and the young royal family stepped from their carriages. Followed by the king's guards, they walked a few steps across the courtyard and disappeared through a door at the center of the palace. Still, the crowd waited, whispering. Despite the warm day, I started to tremble and could not stop. Minutes passed. As I wondered why we waited there, a set of central balcony doors on the upper level opened, and the king stepped forward.

Deafening cheers erupted from the crowd. "The

Sun King reigns! Long live the king!"

"The king's quarters," Françoise said in my ear, nearly shouting. "From his apartments, he can see the courtyard and keep an eye on his courtiers. Too many attempts were made on his life as a young boy, which is why he is always cautious. Years ago, he moved the court from Paris to better keep an eye on the tongue-wagging courtiers and watch their every move."

I nodded, hoping this wasn't Françoise's way of warning me, as Madame de Maintenon had. I was trying hard to understand her words, but everything was beginning to pour off the roof of my brain. I kept glancing at Françoise, hoping not to lose sight of her.

My head ached. The cheering continued, deafening in volume. I took in the crowd's clothing: low-cut gowns, lacy shirt cuffs, gold-trimmed frocks, hats and shoes with bows and buckles and colorful feathers. I could see every detail in perfect clarity, but somehow the crowd and the palace seemed like a giant veil. Through it, all I could see was the woman begging for bread and the two peasant children, trampled by the king's royal coach.

5 Madame's Dogs

Eventually, the king disappeared, the crowd dispersed, and I followed Françoise across the field of cobblestone and into the south wing of the palace. As she led the way, I craned my neck to take in the blur of tapestries and paintings of angels and mythic heroes. Even the hallways brimmed with statues and intricately carved and gilded furniture. Despite the elegant surroundings, the air was warm and close, drenched with scents of strong perfume and putrid body odors. I longed for a breath of fresh air.

The palace was like a bustling city with walls that closed in around me. I was desperate to get back outside where I could see the sky. I feared I might get lost among the servants, soldiers, and courtiers, never to be found again. I grabbed Françoise's hand

as she led me through yet another crowded room.

At last, Françoise stopped outside a set of doors. Rather than knock, she scratched her finger—her littlest fingernail grown long, as I learned, for just this purpose—on one of the double doors, and then opened them into a room with light blue drapes, chairs, couches, and bed curtains. Here, the air was fresh. Sunlight flowed in through long windows opened to a flower-filled courtyard. I breathed deeply, relieved to be away from clamoring crowds.

Madame sat at a small table beside a window and barely glanced up from her writing. "Cécile, Françoise will introduce you to my dogs." A half dozen tiny dogs surrounded Madame. "You may sit on the floor with them." I was to learn that I would always sit on the floor or stand in Madame's presence, never sit in a chair.

She continued, muttering to herself. "I simply have to write another letter. Along with my coin collecting, it is what I do. I'll write another letter, seal it with wax, and then, like all of my letters, it will be read before it leaves the palace. That old trollop constantly meddles, as if I'm a danger to France—indeed!"

Françoise, who I had guessed was twenty or so, spread her skirts around her as she sat on the floor, and then motioned for me to join her. Gradually, all six dogs rose from their perches and trotted closer to investigate us. They were not much bigger than rabbits, with high-set floppy ears, short noses, and large dark eyes. Many of the paintings I had passed boasted such tiny dogs next to their owners. My father had told me about Continental Toy Spaniels. They were the favorite lap dogs at court, he had said. It struck me that peasants could barely feed and care for their children, and yet nobility could afford to have servants such as me tend their dogs. These worlds were as far apart as day and night. I never had given it much thought before, when my life was as sheltered as a snail in its shell.

"You'll never find more loyal and loving dogs than these, Cécile," Françoise whispered. One by one, she introduced the dogs, who took turns sniffing, jumping up on their little legs, and waiting to get scratched. I held out my hand and let the dogs come to know my scent.

"We'll be good friends," I said, petting the dogs. "You'll see."

The dogs were adorable, and in their company, for the first time since I had passed through the palace gates, I felt myself relax. The dogs, I knew, didn't care a speck about my peasant background or lack of wealth. Satisfied after picking up my scent, the dogs returned to Madame's side, taking their places like the guards at court.

Monsieur Titti, the oldest, had fathered dozens of puppies. His coat, black with a white chest, had lost its sheen. He was the first to greet us and the first to return to Madame at her writing table.

Mademoiselle Minette, a white spaniel with black spots, curled under Madame's skirts. Next came the three *Chars:* Charmille, Charmion, and Charmonte, all of them curly haired and tan. Charmille, the tiniest, settled under Madame's arm; Charmonte lay on the other edge of Madame's skirts; and Charmion began to pace with a high-pitched whine.

"Oh, I see the problem," whispered Françoise, who stood and placed another chair next to Madame's. Charmion stopped whining, hopped up, and curled into a tan ball.

Last came Stabdille. He was the largest of the dogs, his coat was mottled brown and black, and he seemed by far the most intelligent and curious. He sat on another chair at the table and watched Madame with his big brown eyes as she moved her quill pen across paper. Then he glanced back at me, as if to say, *See? I'm doing my job. I hope you do yours.*

6 *Disaster*

While Madame's other servants tended her linens, food, and *toilette* needs, I tended the dogs. Françoise taught me my duties. I learned how to brush the dogs' coats, wipe their noses, and clean their teeth, eyes, and ears with a soft cloth. While Madame wrote, the dogs competed for their favorite spots near her. I sat in the corner, watching and waiting to take the dogs outside.

At night, when the dogs climbed in bed with Madame, I slept on a small bed at the edge of the room, missing my papa, and wishing for the body warmth and the company of the dogs. But the dogs were Madame's, and, though they were gentle creatures, their devotion to her was fierce.

The next afternoon, when the dogs began to

whine, Madame said, "Please take them outside, Cécile. Often, I will join you, but today I must finish this letter."

Françoise rose from the floor, and I did the same. We leashed the dogs and walked with them out of Madame's apartment, down a small staircase, along several halls, and, finally, outside to the grounds behind the palace.

Arm in arm, elaborately dressed ladies and gentlemen with sabers at their sides strolled along pathways between groomed hedges. Couples entwined on stone benches in tiny groves. Here and there, small groups of musicians played, their foreheads sweaty as they leaned over their instruments.

Beyond the palace, a series of large pools— Françoise called it the Grand Canal—fanned into a cross, flanked by trimmed trees, straight as soldiers. Gondolas, skiffs, and even a miniature ship floated on the canal. Everywhere I looked, life-sized statues towered beside paths between flower beds and shady groves of trees. Fountains sprouted dragons, gods, cherubs, and frogs and sent cascades of shimmering water high into the air.

The palace grounds were an intricate maze. Françoise led me around until my head throbbed. When we paused to let the dogs relieve themselves, I asked, "Do you ever get lost?"

"Sometimes, but all the paths lead back— eventually—to the palace. This was once all a swamp," she said. "The king used to come here to a hunting lodge as a child." I could not imagine the king as a child. It seemed he had reigned forever in France. And from the palace to the gardens, the king's message was clear: everything was under his power. I felt as if I had climbed a mountain to a dizzying height and was seeing the world from a new perspective. My footing was uncertain, and I hoped I would never fall from the king's favor.

We paused at the edge of a long stone terrace and glanced down. Below, rows and rows of potted trees filled the courtyard.

"Those are orange trees," Françoise said. "The king loves oranges."

I didn't even know what an orange was. Françoise saw my confusion and said, "You eat them. Or rather, the king eats them."

In the middle of this courtyard, palm trees in giant silver pots skirted a round pool. Beyond the *Orangerie*, another canal filled with racing skiffs stretched south.

A sharp pull on my hand caught my attention. I looked down. To my horror, one of the dogs' collars lay on the ground, empty. And racing away from me, headed toward the nearest fountain, dashed the mottled brown and black dog.

I struggled to remember his name. "Stad—Stud—" I called. Finally, it came to me. "Stabdille!" I shouted.

The little dog didn't listen. Instead, he scampered across the gravel path toward two women, a young child, and a governess pushing a carriage.

Françoise gasped. "Ah, *non*," she whispered. "It's Madame de Maintenon and the princess. Hurry before he gets into trouble. I'll wait with the other dogs. *Allez!* Go!"

I ran. But before I was halfway to the fountain,

Stabdille had reached them and was standing on the hem of Princess Marie-Adélaïde's skirt. She erupted in laughter. "Such a funny little fellow! Aren't you one of Madame's dogs?" She reached down and scratched Stabdille between his floppy ears.

The princess's son hopped up on the edge of the fountain, his sandy hair bouncing on his shoulders. "You can't get me here!" he laughed, jumping up and down to get Stabdille's attention.

"Get down, now," Madame de Maintenon ordered. "That is no way for royalty to behave. You are not at Marly now."

I hurried toward the fountain's edge and closed in on the errant dog. Just as I drew close enough to grab him, Stabdille leaped up beside the boy and placed his paws on the boy's knees.

Madame de Maintenon reached for the boy. I reached for the dog. And in a tangle of arms and feet and legs and paws, the boy and the dog fell into the fountain waters with a mighty splash.

7 *Doctor Fagon*

I leaped into the water to fetch the dog while the governess, old enough to be my grandmother, jumped in after the boy. Dripping wet in her dark gown, she held the child in her sturdy arms. The edge of the boy's forehead was scraped red. He coughed and sputtered out a gulp of water. As the governess sat the boy on the fountain's ledge, I hoisted Stabdille, who looked like a drenched rat, under my arm. My new dress was soaked to my waist.

"I'm so sorry," I began. "I didn't mean—"

Marie-Adélaïde kissed her son on his forehead, sat down beside him, and wiped water from his eyes. "Oh, just a cool swim on a hot afternoon!" she said.

The boy's lower lip trembled. "But Maman, I hurt my head." With his next breath he asked, "Where's

the puppy?" His eyes scanned the path.

His mother kissed him again, then smoothed his wet hair with a brush of her fingers. "You're the king's great-grandson. You'll be fine. And the puppy is really a full-grown dog. He's Madame's, and I'm sure you've met him before. He must remember you. I think he just wanted to be your friend."

Madame de Maintenon did not say a word, but she glared at me. At a tilt of her head, two soldiers trotted toward us across the courtyard. I lowered my gaze.

The soldiers' footsteps loomed closer. I couldn't breathe or move. Would I be sent home that very day, humiliated and ashamed, a dishonor to Papa? What would I tell my father? I couldn't let him

down, not when his greatest wish in the world
was for me to be at the court of Versailles. Perhaps
he wouldn't have wished for such a thing if he had
known how difficult it would be to please everyone.

"At your service, Madame de Maintenon," a soldier
said, bowing low.

"Send a page for Dr. Fagon," she said. "I want him
to examine Bretagne."

Immediately the soldiers set off to the nearest
building, where they spoke with a boy about my
age—a page—who dashed off through the nearest
doorway.

Relief spread through my shoulders. The soldiers
hadn't been coming for me after all. I glanced at
Bretagne, who leaned against his mother's chest.
The princess stroked her son's long, sandy curls.
His forehead was scraped and bumped, but no worse
than I had received tromping through the forest and
stumbling over roots. I could hear my father say,
"Nothing that a little rest won't heal."

Madame de Maintenon turned to me. "You are
Madame's new charge. If Bretagne is hurt in any

serious way, I will hold Madame accountable."

With a deep bow of my head and an even deeper curtsy, I tried to apologize. Then I found my voice. "I am terribly sorry, Madame de Maintenon. I only meant to fetch Stabdille, who darted off on his own." I looked at the boy, who was watching the dog squirm under my arm.

"He wants to be my friend," Bretagne said, reaching toward the dog.

"You have plenty of friends," Madame de Maintenon said. "The whole *Ménagerie* of animals," she said, sweeping her arm toward the south wing of the Grand Canal—"is for your enjoyment."

"Put him down so I may pet him," Bretagne said.

I looked from Madame de Maintenon to Marie-Adélaïde, who smiled and nodded. "Yes, that's a fine idea."

I stepped closer and placed Stabdille at the feet of Bretagne. The little dog wagged his tail so fiercely that I thought it might fall off. Bretagne bent forward and scratched the dog between his ears. "Did you like the water?" he whispered. "I did."

He asked the dog's name, and I told him.

"I will be king someday," Bretagne said, stroking one of the dog's ears and then the other. His manner hovered somewhere between the gaiety of a child and the somberness of a future king. "Then you will have to bring Stabdille to me whenever I ask for him."

"Of course," I said with a bow, but a thought struck me and a laugh escaped my lips.

"What's so funny?" the boy said, his eyes meeting mine.

"King Louis appears to never grow old," I said, carefully choosing my words. "Since your parents will be our next king and queen, your time on the throne likely will come when you're much, much older. Would you then have me dig up this poor dog when you ask for him?" I asked, smiling—and praying he would understand my joke.

"Then," the boy said cunningly, half-closing his eyes, "as king, I would command you to bring him to life again."

"As you wish," I said, eyes downcast and taking in not only the princess's fine brocaded silk skirts, but the boy's wet skirts as well.

"Yes, if only life were that simple," Marie-Adélaïde chimed in, her voice as lilting and heart-warming as a melody.

"What's your name?" Bretagne asked.

"My name is Cécile Revel," I answered.

"Revel?" came a deep voice. I turned and curtsied swiftly to the man who had suddenly appeared. Beneath a dark, shoulder-length wig stood a man as skinny as a wooden rake. Dark whiskers protruded from the nostrils of his thin, long nose. He stared at me with eyes like olives. "We had a doctor of the same name here years ago—"

His words stopped me. A doctor who had the same name?

". . . shipped off to the *Bastille*," he said, gesturing with his forefinger for me to move away from the boy, who was busy chirping praises to the little dog.

The Bastille? The very word made me shudder. The Bastille was the prison in Paris where criminals, prisoners, and enemies of the king were sent and never heard from again. Rumors about the prison spread across the countryside. Some said the prison kept its prisoners in royal comfort, while others repeated stories of torture. In either case, its prisoners were locked tightly away, and many never left. I drew myself up as tall as the fountain's pillar of shooting water. What matter did it make that another doctor named Revel had once been at court? The doctor mentioned could not have been my father. And sent to the Bastille? Impossible. Still, a chill darted like a minnow through the churning waters of my mind.

At the stone ledge by the Orangerie, Françoise waited with the other dogs. I caught her eye and she mine. I shrugged my shoulders, hoping to show her that I wanted to leave, but I had to wait to be excused.

"May I take the dog now?" I asked.

Bretagne peered up and sternly shook his head. Then he bent over Stabdille again, who was stretched on his back, paws up, at the boy's feet.

I waited.

"Let me examine you, young sir," Dr. Fagon said, nudging the dog aside with his shoe.

"Don't bleed me," the boy pleaded.

My father called the common treatment of blood-letting "complete and absolute lunacy," and he refused to treat patients with a scalpel, except to lance a boil or remove a badly infected limb. "Never take away something useful and necessary to the body, like blood," he would say.

"No, not for this," the doctor replied. "The regular bleedings you receive already serve to keep you fit enough."

If regular bleedings were part of being royal, I was glad for the moment that I was of more humble beginnings.

Dr. Fagon opened his physician's case on the edge of the fountain and withdrew a round glass with an ivory handle. He put the glass tool close to the boy's wound.

"What's that?" the boy asked.

"My new magnifying glass, young prince. It makes objects appear larger," he said. "Yes, it's a slight injury, and in this heat we don't want it to fester." He pulled out a small tin of ointment and applied a gray paste to Bretagne's forehead. Then he wiped his hands on a small cloth and clapped his skinny hands together. "Done."

Marie-Adélaïde nodded to the doctor, rose, and helped Bretagne to his feet. "Thank you, Dr. Fagon," she said. She motioned with a tilt of her thick auburn curls—her own and not a wig—to Madame de Maintenon. "Time for our visit with Grandpapa," she said.

They set off, the governess trailing water from her dark skirts as she pushed the carriage after them. The toddler must have slept the whole time, for I hadn't heard him peep.

Before Stabdille could run away again, I quickly gathered him in my arms.

Dr. Fagon closed his case and glanced at me quizzically. "You have that doctor's eyes—rather serious, a bit close together. And you say your name is—"

"Begging your leave, Monsieur," I said, pretending not to hear. Before he could say another word, I curtsied and hurried back to Françoise's side.

8 *Endless Etiquette*

September whirled by. My days were spent learning etiquette and the daily routines of court life. I could hardly believe that the public watched the king rise from his four-poster bed every morning and go through his morning toilette, where one nobleman handed him a shirt, another his shoes, and on and on, each hoping to find favor with the king.

Most requests to the king were made midmorning when he strolled down the long Hall of Mirrors. Huge mirrors lined one wall of the room, while the other side boasted full-length windows overlooking the Grand Canal. The Hall was always packed with courtiers dressed as bright as peacocks. Men wore shoes with high heels, often painted red like the king's, with silk stockings, breeches, and brocaded topcoats. Women wore dresses that cinched their waists and left their shoulders and necks bare. I often stood behind Madame with the dogs.

"Marly, Sire?" one man asked, hoping to join the king on his next hunting trip to Marly and have the chance to be closer to His Highness.

Another would ask for money to cover gambling debts from the night before, for every evening the card tables hummed with activity.

And still another hopeful courtier would ask again, "Marly, Sire?"

I had thought life at Versailles would be heaven, but for those who lived at the palace and whose lives revolved around the king, escaping with him to the countryside seemed their highest goal.

The king's answers usually came with a slight nod or shake of his head.

After the assembly in the Hall of Mirrors came mass in the beautiful chapel the king had built within the palace. Going to mass was one of my few breaks from tending the dogs. Under a brilliantly painted domed ceiling, the congregation sat and stood on the main level, and the king, the royal family, and important members of the court sat in the galleries above.

Every day, while the priest delivered his sermon, Madame snored loudly enough for me to hear her all the way in the back, where I stood. She couldn't help it, she had told me.

"As soon as the sermon starts, I promptly fall asleep," she had said.

I tried to listen, as the priests often preached about feeding the hungry, clothing the naked, and showing kindness to strangers—good words to live by, I thought—though from what I had seen of life already, I doubted that many at court took the sermons to heart. Mass often lasted over an hour—sometimes two or three hours—and my legs ached from standing. During those times, I almost wished I were a dog so I could curl up and nap.

In the afternoons, I roamed the grounds with the dogs. Madame accompanied me when she wasn't hunting with the king's party. One warm and sunny day, Madame and I rode with the dogs in a gondola to the south wing of the Grand Canal.

"The Ménagerie," Madame explained, wrestling with her heavy skirts to get out of the gondola, "was the king's gift to Marie-Adélaïde." Not only was this my chance to see a carousel for the first time, but Françoise had explained earlier that the Ménagerie housed exotic animals and birds from other lands: elephants, giraffes, lions, ostriches, flamingos, and many other creatures I could neither name nor imagine. The fields stretching beyond the Ménagerie provided room for the herds of animals to graze.

"Does the king raise them for food?" I asked, as we wandered through the Ménagerie.

Madame laughed. "Oh no, Cécile. It's all for enjoyment. The king built it for the princess when she arrived at court. She was your age then."

My mind swam at the thought. Had this world been given to me, I wondered if I would be a completely different girl. Already the princess's son demanded what he wanted, expecting the world to serve him. I tried to shrug off my thoughts. My duty was to serve. Still, my mind wrestled with such ideas, just as it wrestled with the sight of the startling animals before me.

All too soon, we turned away from the animals and headed back to the palace on foot.

Madame huffed. "The animals are somewhat like the exotic creatures at the palace, don't you think?"

I laughed. "Oui, Madame," I said, for the palace certainly was filled not only with outlandishly styled courtiers but also with visiting foreigners from as far away as China and the New World.

"Exotic creatures locked up with no way of escaping," she added. "I hear talk that our French ships are manned by captives and criminals who are chained below the decks, forced to row as galley slaves until they die. Imagine. Well, sometimes I think there is no greater slavery than to be here at the palace in lifelong service to the king."

To this, I only nodded. Such a bold comment frightened me. I might think such a thing, but I would never dare to say it aloud. If I did, I might lose my position—or worse.

Madame had already told me more than once

how she longed to return to her native Germany to see her family. But each time she asked, her request was denied. She had married the king's brother, who had died ten years earlier, but her duty, as a member of the royal family, was to remain in the company of the king. If the king went to Marly or Fontainebleau, so did the royal family, and so did Madame. She had never been able to return home—and with a war being waged for a tenth year against her homeland, there was almost no chance of her seeing her own family again.

"And you, do you miss your papa, Cécile?" Madame asked me.

Her question startled me. It was unexpected, like dropping a bucket into an abandoned well and coming up with water. I nodded but looked straight ahead as we walked, for I did not want to shed the tears that had rushed to my eyes. I had lived with my father, helped him clean and cook, and studied under his direction, but I hadn't realized the depths of my feelings for him until I left. I longed to sit by our hearth and listen to his soothing voice as he told stories he'd heard about court, or read from the *Iliad* or the *Odyssey*. Now, more than anything, it was his voice I missed. I shrugged, my shoulder muscles tight. "Yes, some," I said. If I told Madame how I truly felt, perhaps she would think I wasn't strong enough to be at court.

We strolled, and I managed to keep the leashes straight by holding three dogs with one hand and three with the other.

At an arched stone trellis topped by urns, we stopped. The dogs paused and stretched out in a slight rim of shade next to a fountain. In the fountain's center, water spurted from the mouth of a giant who was crushed beneath a rain of rocks.

"From a Greek myth," Madame explained. "The giant made the mistake of going against Zeus."

My father had taught me mythology, so I knew that Zeus was the greatest of the Greek gods.

"For challenging Zeus," she continued, "the giant was buried beneath stones."

"I see," I said. I thought I knew how that giant felt under all that weight. Ever since I had arrived at the palace, my neck and head had felt tight with worry over making a mistake. I wanted to do my duty and be a good servant—and thereby honor my father, Madame, and the Sun King. But I was coming to know duty as a crushing yoke upon my shoulders.

9 A Season of Rain

That afternoon, when we returned with the dogs to the apartment, I gathered my courage. "Madame, about the doctors here," I began, hoping to inquire about the Dr. Revel who once had served at court.

"If more people took walks and got fresh air," Madame said, jumping into a topic about which she clearly had opinions, "there would be less illness at the palace. But so many French—I will always be a German and not understand them—worry that the outside air is not good for them. Did you know that many of the women at court have little dark corners built for them in the palace where they can go and rest? If they stepped outside and got a little exercise, they wouldn't be so ill—and they might be able to tighten the waists on their dresses, besides."

"Madame," I asked. "Did you know a Dr. Revel who once worked here? Madame de Maintenon and Dr. Fagon said he had been sent away to the Bastille."

Madame paused, tilted her head to look at me, and tapped her well-padded cheek with her fingers. "Yes," she said. "A man of deep convictions. Like me, he believed in fresh air, brisk walks and exercise, and drinking lots of fresh water. He spoke up against many of the practices at court that tend to kill people off more than help them. He was a good man who stood up for his beliefs." Then she stopped, finished with the conversation.

"I see." I stored her words away but came to no conclusions. And I knew better than to press her for more right then.

That afternoon the weather changed. Rain began to fall in a soft drizzle, and it didn't stop for weeks. Before long, mildew grew in the halls and corners of the palace, and moods soured. Even Madame's dogs put their noses outside and balked at going out. I had to tug them after me.

I spent many hours on a cushion on the floor, not

much different than a well-trained dog, except that during my free hours, I read novels (loaned to me by Madame) and wrote letters. I wrote to my father several times, telling him everything about life at Versailles. I wrote about the doctor who had been sent to the Bastille, and I asked Papa if he had a brother or a relative with the same name who once had been at court. I wrote about the dogs and asked for advice when one of the dog's eyelids became crusty and when another scratched at a troublesome ear until it bled. He wrote back with advice, but he never answered my question about the banished doctor.

One afternoon, a page delivered a note to Madame's apartment. Françoise delivered the note to Madame, who read it to me. "'Please send Stabdille. Bretagne says he will study today only if he can see the little dog first.'"

Looking up from the note, Madame said, "What the boy wants, the boy gets. Have you noticed? Under Madame de Maintenon's rule, the policy is to spoil children, not to discipline them when they sorely need it. May as well let good fruit go to rot. Well, I suppose we have no choice, Cécile," she said. She nodded to me. "You may take Stabdille. The other dogs will keep me company."

I hoped the page would wait and show me how to find my way to Marie-Adélaïde's apartments. When I stepped out with Stabdille under my arm, the page was there waiting for me.

Brown-eyed, and about my age, he held his chin high. "This way," he said. He was long-legged and his narrow shoulder blades were tucked back like wings.

I followed close behind him. His tailored jacket fell above his knees. In blue stockings and thick, two-inch heels, he strode ahead while I struggled to keep up, my free hand holding my skirt hem from the floor. Still, I was happy to be with someone closer to my age, even for a short time. "Do you live here at court, too?" I asked.

He didn't turn his head. "No, all pages live, train, and study in quarters above the stables."

"When I first arrived," I said, "I thought the stables were the palace."

"Me too," he said, confiding in me with a quick glance over his shoulder. His teeth were uneven, but his eyes sparked with intelligence. "I came from the country. I had never dreamed of such a place."

I nodded. "My dreams were—well, simple. Real life is never exactly like a dream, is it?"

He pushed his shoulders back and kept walking.

"What do you study?" I asked, thinking pages probably learned how to ride a horse at high speed to deliver a message to the battlefront, and such things.

"Along with horse handling and etiquette, I study science, literature, history, and mathematics. It's boring, but if I'm good at my studies, perhaps I could become Master of the Horse someday."

"There are no such places for girls to study," I said.

"Except for St. Cyr," he said.

"What's that?"

"A school for girls—at least, for girls of nobility."

Such a place was not in my future, which would lie in serving at court—if I made no mistakes. I saw my life stretching like a long, straight, unbending road. Madame had said something about there being no escape. But escape to what? I was not ready to think about marriage. A life as a servant to Madame was the best I could hope for, and I was grateful for her many kindnesses to me.

The page led me over a marble floor of black and white squares and finally up the wide staircase to the queen's apartments, which, as the future queen, Marie-Adélaïde occupied. The princess was already, in the minds of nearly everyone in France, the next beloved queen. Though her husband, the Duc de Bourgogne, would become the next king, he was quieter and more industrious than his wife, who drew crowds everywhere she went. Everyone who saw her seemed to fall under the spell of her engaging smile and melodic laughter—especially the king and Madame de Maintenon.

With a nod, the page said, "If you need me—I mean, if you need anything—my name is Philippe." He bowed. "At your service," he added, his face flushing as he scratched on the door and then quickly turned away.

I nearly laughed out loud. Poor Philippe was, I had

to admit to myself, being flirtatious with me. All the romances and affairs of court must have gone to his head. Maybe he thought I was someone important. Certainly he didn't realize I was only a servant of dogs.

I dropped my smile and forced a more serious expression on my face as the door opened. Then I stepped into a room so gilded that I almost squinted, even though rain fell in gray sheets outside the windows.

I curtsied to a cluster of women in a semicircle of chairs. On the woven carpet rested a miniature sedan chair, an ornate box with a door, enclosing a tiny velvet chair. Through its glass windows, Bretagne stared at me and then smiled.

Marie-Adélaïde called to me from the center of the group. "His tutor stormed away," she said. "Bretagne has locked himself in until he sees that dog again. Thank you for bringing him to us."

I curtsied, then led Stabdille closer. I kneeled beside the sedan's window and lifted him to the glass. Nose to nose, the boy and dog said hello.

Stabdille's tail wagged wildly.

"See?" Bretagne said, his voice muffled. "You brought him when I asked for him!" He unbolted the side door, pushed it open, and stretched out his hands. "Stabdille wants to go for a ride with me. We're going to go far, far away, and no one will ever find us again."

"Of course," I said, and handed over the dog, who immediately licked Bretagne's face. Then the boy snapped the door shut, the dog in his lap.

I sat down on the floor beside them, waiting. For a long time, Bretagne sang as he played with the dog. An hour or so passed, and I pretended not to listen to the women's conversation as they embroidered and gossiped together.

"If she wouldn't eat so much—"

"Eat? You mean, if she wouldn't *drink* so much."

"She's such a glutton. Even the doctor's purges can't remedy her overeating."

When the boy's tutor stepped in and loudly placed books upon a table, Bretagne kissed Stabdille on his nose, opened the sedan door, and handed him back to me. Then he walked over to his tutor, who bowed to the boy.

I stood with the dog under my arm, ready to be dismissed.

"Cécile," Madame de Maintenon said from the group, a forced smile rising on her face. "By the way, where did your father learn his medical training that allowed him to help Madame when she took her fall last summer?"

"I don't know," I replied. And that was the truth. My father's life had been filled with secrets and missing pieces that now made me yearn to know the whole of his past.

"When a certain Dr. Revel served here—" she said.

"As Second Physician," another added.

". . . some called him brilliant," Madame de Maintenon continued. "Most called him a lunatic. The king had to send him away."

I didn't move a muscle in my face or limbs, but my stomach squirmed.

The women stared at me, as if waiting for an answer, even though I hadn't heard a question. I had the strong sense that I had been their topic of speculation and gossip before. A velvet curtain of silence hung heavily.

"But my papa is at home," I blurted. "The doctor you speak of was sent to the Bastille."

Madame de Maintenon nodded. "True, but Dr. Revel was given a sentence of a mere eighteen months and banished from the palace, never to return."

"Cécile," Marie-Adélaïde asked kindly. "Is it possible this man is your father?"

Of course he could be the same physician. In my bones, I knew this to be true. All the pieces were fitting together and becoming clear. Papa had served at court, where he had acquired his knowledge about court life. Then he had been sent to the Bastille. After he was released, he must have gone to live quietly in Rileaux, where I was born. I felt betrayed. Neither Maman nor Papa had ever told me the truth. I pictured my father now, a younger man, spouting off his opinions as he often did at home. That he had spoken his mind at court, regardless of the cost, did not surprise me. But I would not let his past mistakes become my undoing.

"No," I said. "My father is a peasant, nothing more." My words poured out of me like water from a vase, leaving behind a deep and hollow emptiness.

"Good," Madame de Maintenon said, glancing up from her needlework. "Otherwise I feared that your mind might be tainted by wrong thinking. To go against the court physicians is to go against the king."

"My duty is to serve the king and his court," I said with a deep curtsy, nearly dropping Stabdille, who clawed my arm with his hind nails, desperate to get free.

Madame de Maintenon nodded, and this time a genuine smile spread across her smooth, white face. "Very well, then, Cécile. *Très bien.* You may go."

Everything they said made sense. Of course Papa was Dr. Revel. I turned away, stepped into the hall, and hung my head, ashamed that I had been so quick to protect my position and to deny my own father.

10 *The Letter*

In late November, snow fell in wet clumps and spread a cover as thick as my goose-down quilt over Versailles.

With my wool cape around my shoulders, I led the dogs outside. They gingerly lifted their tiny paws, hesitant to step outside—just like many of the women at court, who feared that the slightest breeze might mess up their piled hair, white face paint, and rouge. Madame refused to follow this fashion and said the women looked like white rabbits with their ears pulled back.

"Go ahead," I said to the dogs. They sniffed the snow and lifted their feet as if they were dancing a minuet. "A little snow won't hurt you."

The air was sweet with moisture, and I prayed

the sun wouldn't appear too quickly and melt the snow away. I glanced around. The grounds—to my delight—were nearly empty for the first time since I had arrived three months earlier.

Stabdille was the first to eat the snow, and the others followed his lead. When he began to pull at his leash, jumping up and down on his hind legs, I gave in and with the dogs set off running—something frowned upon at court—across the slippery grounds. I couldn't help myself. We raced through the snow between white groves of trees, around empty fountains layered in white, and past statues with white wigs. Twice I slipped and fell, my legs going right out from under my skirts. The dogs were quick to cover me with wet kisses. I laughed out loud.

Finally, snow clumped so thickly around the dogs' furry legs that they became as burdened as oxen, and I had to carry the oldest, Monsieur Titti, back to the palace.

That evening, when Madame and Françoise were gone, I heard two short scratches, then one long one at the door.

I pushed the dogs aside, rose from my pillow, and opened the double doors. Philippe, the page, held a letter in his hand.

"Madame is not in, but she will return soon," I replied.

"The letter is for you," he said, and flinched. "I'm afraid the news is not good."

"How do you know?" I snatched the letter from him. Madame had complained regularly about her mail being opened and read, but why would anyone bother to read mine? Maybe I truly was suspected of being a spy, or of having been sent to poison someone at court. Ridiculous. "Were you asked to read my letter?"

He shook his head. "No, not I. But I was told

about—" He paused, looked at me, and tilted his head. "I'm sorry, Cécile."

I closed the door in his face, leaned my back against it, and tore open the letter, its wax seal poorly refastened. The short letter was not from my father, but from the priest at my village church. It read:

> *My dear Cécile,*
> *I write to you with sad news. Your father died of smallpox. He was given last rites before his soul went to be with Our Lord, and he was buried one week ago here at Saint Augustine's cemetery.*
> *May God be with you.*

I read the words over and over and over, hoping that I might change their meaning, but the letter was a sword, thrust into my heart and piercing me to its hilt. My mind ached, struggling to comprehend. I had heard of a recent smallpox outbreak in Paris, but I had never imagined it would travel so quickly to the countryside. Papa's cough had no doubt left him too weak to battle this illness. And I had not been at his side. Had I been there, had I given him chamomile tea or broth, perhaps he would have survived. My mind raced with questions. What were his last hours like? Had he been all alone? Had anyone been there to comfort him, as he had comforted and helped so many others? I needed to know more about him, and now I would never be able to ask him what I needed to know. I needed to hear his voice, and to thank him for the hours he'd spent teaching me to read and write. And, with the terrible news of Papa's death, every detail of my mother's death came back to me as well, like embers heaped upon embers. I could feel myself once again lying beside her in her bed as she struggled for her last breath, while tears flowed down my face.

I pressed my back against the door.

"Cécile?" Philippe asked, and scratched again at the door.

"Go away," I said. "Please."

"I'll come back tomorrow," he said. "I'm sorry." His footsteps faded away.

I felt myself being pitched over the edge of a steep

cliff, twirling and tumbling into darkness. I had
dreamed of finding heaven at Versailles, but those
had been the dreams of a complete and utter fool.
I had failed to understand all the goodness, the true
wealth that was once under my own roof, with my
father. Each day together had been my bag of gold
coins. We struggled and we were poor, but we had
each other.

More footsteps came toward the door, the clicking
of Madame's and Françoise's heels.

I gulped a deep breath, tucked the letter beneath
my cushion on the floor, and returned to brushing
the dogs. They scampered around me and licked
my face and hands, somehow aware of my pain
and doing what they could to comfort me.

Chattering, Madame stepped in, followed by
Françoise. "But look at Cécile. She's young. She has
her life—a future—ahead of her. At my age, I ask,
what does it truly matter if I am poisoned to death?"

I didn't look up from my pillow on the floor, but
kept brushing. I had learned that Madame did not
always want me to answer her questions, but rather

she simply wanted an audience. My eyes began to blur with tears. I brushed one of the dogs too hard and she cowered away from me with a whimper. "Forgive me, Charmonte," I whispered, kissing her head and petting her back.

"Is it so important to the future of France whether I live or die?" Madame continued. "Every bite I take is watched, lest I be poisoned or lest I choke. God will take my life when He is ready, and there is nothing anyone can do to add a moment to my life or shorten it, unless it is by His will. I have come to despise eating alone while being watched by a standing audience. It simply takes all the pleasure from a meal."

Madame was large and round-bellied. I knew she hadn't lost all pleasure in eating. "Welcome back, Madame," I managed, but my voice was shaky. "Your dogs have missed you."

I gave Stabdille one last brush and a quick kiss on the top of his head, then let him race with the rest of the dogs to their places. I knew the routine, and so did the dogs: Madame would write one more letter before going with Françoise to the theater. Tonight's play was by the famous writer Molière, who was a favorite of the king. Usually I wished I could go along, but tonight I was relieved to stay behind.

"Are you going to eat?" Françoise asked, but I shook my head. Usually, I raced with anticipation through the maze of hallways and stairs to the kitchens, where I sat at a long table with other servants. I never went away hungry, even though other servants often grumbled that times were lean. From time to time, we ate leftovers from the king's banquets—everything from pheasant and salmon to caramel peaches and gooseberry-currant jam. But today my appetite had died along with my father.

"I'm here to watch the dogs, Cécile," Françoise continued. "You're free to go."

I could not look up to meet her eyes. I could scarcely move.

Madame shifted in her chair. "Cécile," she said, "is something the matter?"

Reluctantly, I reached under the cushion. I held up the crumpled letter. Madame motioned for me to bring it to her, which I did. She read the note and handed it to Françoise.

"Oh, Cécile," Madame said, tears melting in her ice-blue eyes. She held out her arms to me, and that's when I started to cry.

11 *Doctor Revel, My Father*

The following day, after mass, Françoise helped loosen the stays on Madame's dress, which was woven in a pattern of ferns and flowers and edged with lace and pearls.

"Will there be anything else for now, Madame?" she asked.

"No, feel free to go, Françoise. I have several letters to finish today."

Françoise left. Madame sat at her writing desk, and I stretched out on my small bed. The dogs took up their afternoon napping posts, except Stabdille. He planted his four legs squarely on the table, pointing his square nose at Madame and wagging his tail.

I watched him from under my goose-down quilt, chin on my crossed arms, wishing for sleep to fall on me like a boulder. Instead, thoughts of my father filled my head and kept me wide awake. How could I be my "father's pride," as he had last called me, when I had denied him? I had even said out loud that he was a peasant and nothing more, as if he were worthless. What did money and position matter? Papa had been the kindest and most generous man on earth. I didn't deserve to be his daughter.

Madame spoke up. "Cécile, I do believe Stabdille would like to visit Bretagne today."

"Oh, Madame," I began in protest. I wished I could complain of arthritis as Madame often did, or say that my knees were bad, so that I couldn't do anything but stay on my narrow bed and sleep for days on end. But I held my tongue, hoping she would think I was ill.

Stabdille jumped up on his hind legs and barked. "See? He says 'oui' to my idea. His thoughts exactly."

"Perhaps he has too much energy and would be a trouble today," I said.

"Far too much energy to stay here," said Madame. "He and young Bretagne will make a good match."

"But he might disturb the princess or Madame de

Maintenon." I knew I was risking being disobedient. I wanted to serve and please Madame, but my stomach churned at the thought of having to speak to anyone, especially "the old trollop," as Madame often called Madame de Maintenon, who might ask me more questions about my poor papa. By now, Madame de Maintenon would know of my father's death. She may have read the letter herself. Nothing at court slipped past her.

Madame wrote a note, tucked it in an envelope, and held it toward me between her fingers. "Give this to the nearest page," she said. "It will alert Marie-Adélaïde that you will be on your way soon—after the dogs have their afternoon stroll."

I was not going to change her mind, nor was I going to win her sympathy. On heavy legs, I rose to my feet and straightened my dress. Before I could take another breath, I had to speak up. "Madame," I began, my voice wavering. "Please tell me the truth about my father. I cannot bear to be tortured with questions yet again and feel that Madame de Maintenon knows more than I do about my papa."

Madame looked at me and set the envelope on her table next to Stabdille, who was circling after his tail. Finally, he settled with a sigh into a ball beside Madame's inkwell.

Leaning on her elbows, Madame paused and gazed out the window.

I waited silently. In the flower bed beyond, the snow had melted, revealing plants that were gray and withered from the first frost.

Madame asked, "You want the truth, do you?" She touched her fingers tip to tip.

Did I really want the truth? Part of me wanted to know all of it, while part of me wanted to live with my memories as they were. But I had lived with mysteries about my father for too long. I nodded, suddenly timid at her serious tone and what I might learn.

"Then come closer."

I stepped beside her table.

"As you have likely guessed, your father was the very doctor who was sent away. And yes, we recognized each other in the forest that day." She glanced up at me. "I had the greatest respect for your father, but I could do nothing to save him from the decision of the king. When your father spoke out bravely against Dr. Fagon, accusing him of using methods that killed my husband, the king had no choice but to banish him."

"Your husband?" I repeated in disbelief. Straight and tall, I listened. Nothing could have made me move as Madame spoke.

She nodded, and continued. "Monsieur, my husband, was a frail man—unlike his brother, the king—and yet he lived a wild and reckless life. We were at Marly. I had a four-hour bout with fever. Monsieur told me he was off to dine, as he was hungry. 'You are ill,' he told me. 'Go back to your room.' A mere half hour later, Madame de Ventadour, who is now Bretagne's governess, came into my room, white as a sheet, and told me that my husband was not well.

"I ran to Monsieur's room, and His Grace was conscious but barely able to speak. Yet he said to me once again, 'You are ill. Go back to your room.'

Imagine—my husband said those words to me when he was deathly ill himself. But I wouldn't go. I refused to leave his side.

"Soon the doctors were bustling about in the room. Dr. Fagon was giving orders, and your father was there as Second Physician. Your father and I had often talked about health and medicine, and we agreed on many points. He had told me that he didn't believe that bloodletting helped, but that night, he held his tongue; he knew such accepted methods would not be changed easily or quickly. At my husband's bedside, with their war chest of knives, the doctors bled Monsieur two times, then gave him eleven ounces of emetic and three whole bottles of *gouttes d'Angleterre*—all to no avail. By six in the morning, my husband had taken a turn for the worse. When Dr. Fagon called for the third round of bloodletting, your father spoke up, unable to control his rage. His words still ring in my ears. 'Stop! Enough!' he shouted. 'With each ounce of blood you remove, Monsieur's life slips away. Can you not see that you're killing him?'

"Dr. Fagon wouldn't listen. He ordered your father to be silent. But your father would not be still. Just as Dr. Fagon was ready to begin bleeding my husband's other arm, Dr. Revel—your father—grabbed Fagon's knife and flung it across the room. The tools crashed from the bed to the floor. He shouted, 'I will not allow you to kill off the royal family!'

"At that point, still quite ill myself, I nearly swooned and was forcibly dragged out of the room and put to bed. Cécile, that was the last time I saw your father." Madame paused, looking beyond the window as if she were seeing into another lifetime.

"I suspected the worst, and only later did I learn about his banishment. When anyone is sent to the Bastille, he is usually whisked away in darkness and secrecy."

A chill shuddered through me. I pictured soldiers entering my father's apartment in the dark hours of night, gagging him, and forcing him from the palace.

"My husband died that day at noon, leaving me penniless and completely dependent upon the king's favor. That was just over ten years ago."

Ten years ago. My heart nearly stopped.

"Madame, are you sure? This all happened only ten years ago?"

She smiled forgivingly at me. "Yes, I'm sure, Cécile. I'm getting old, but 1701 is a year I will not forget."

"Madame, but I'm twelve now. My parents said I had been born in Rileaux. I would have been two years old when my father was banished from court. Then . . . I must have been born here."

Madame studied me.

"Why didn't my parents tell me the truth?"

"Perhaps to spare you from expecting too much, from expecting more than life was likely going to offer you," she said gently. "To spare you from disappointment in them."

"But they lied—"

"More importantly," Madame said, "your parents were good people, so unlike many here at court who live only for the next pleasure and entertainment. I'm sure they loved you as much as any parent could and gave you all that you really needed."

I tried to keep up with what she was telling me. "And my mother. What can you tell me?"

"Not much. I met her once, briefly. She was fair-haired, from Normandy, and from what I know, which is precious little, her noble family had fallen into financial disgrace. A match with a doctor, your father, was below her station, but it was a workable marriage for her. That's all I know."

I began to cry, and muffled my sobs in my sleeve. "I'm sorry. I cannot seem to stop."

Madame picked up the envelope addressed to Marie-Adélaïde. She held it in front of me and ripped it in half. "The king believes no one should cry and grieve in public. He likes to see a merry court. I know how it feels to lose those you care about. I thought it might cheer you to go out, but I see I am wrong. Stay here. Sleep, if you wish." She patted the top of Stabdille's head. "You and Cécile will visit Bretagne another day."

12 *The Coming Ball*

After I learned about my father, time flowed as slow as cold honey. Somehow, I filled my days with caring for the dogs and listening to Madame, and eventually November gave way to December.

When Madame learned that I had the ability to read a word and remember its spelling, she said, "Cécile, as long as you can respect my desire for privacy, I will ask you to read my letters from time to time—those I write in French, that is—to make sure my spelling is correct. Then, when the old trollop reads my letters, she may not like my opinions, but at least she won't be able to mock my spelling."

"I'll try, Madame," I said. And I soon discovered that reading Madame's letters was like reading novels or hearing Papa's stories about court life. Madame wrote about her dogs, the king, the courtiers, and the operas, plays, and concerts at court. She wrote about the Huguenots who were tormented and forced out of the country for not following the Catholic faith. She wrote about the shortage of money at court and how the streets of Paris were filled with beggars "black with hunger." She wrote about the long war with Germany and how it hurt her deeply to think of smoke rising from her destroyed homeland, which the king had claimed, all in Madame's name. She wrote about her family and how she longed to see them again, and about the loneliness of life at court. I learned that in the midst of great wealth, she owned very little herself. Françoise, as first lady-in-waiting, owned all of Madame's dresses and inherited them

when Madame got new ones. The first chambermaid, not Madame, owned all the linens, as well as
the nightgowns and petticoats that Madame wore.

I was careful to read her letters and comment only
on misspelled words, not on her thoughts. I never
asked her questions about her letters, either, for fear
that she would think I was too nosy. In truth, her
letters gave me a detailed education about court
life—sometimes more than I wanted to know. And
one night, after studying a letter by candlelight, I
realized that in the emptiness left by my father's
death, I was coming to love Madame, who had
taken me in and given me a home. She could never
replace my maman or papa, but she was as good as
any grandmother could be.

One evening, when wind whipped freezing rain
against the windowpanes and the fire burned logs
faster than they could warm the room, I was reading
a letter for spelling errors. The candelabra was lit and
I was alone, as Madame and Françoise were at the
opera, which Madame said always put her to sleep.

I was stretched out on the sofa, the dogs piled on

top of me from my legs to my chest, helping to keep me warm. Scratches—two short and one long—sounded at the door. The dogs groaned as I moved them into a pile on the end of the sofa, then swung my feet to the floor. Something about the scratching was different—hesitant, extra slow, and drawn out. Ever since Madame had told me about my father, I had been having nightmares of soldiers coming in the middle of the night and dragging me away to the Bastille. More than once, I woke up sweating, then cried silently for my father.

Hesitantly, I turned the gilded handle and pushed open the doors. In the hallway, his face illuminated by a single candle in its holder, stood Philippe. Over the past two months, he had grown two inches taller and his shoulders had grown wider. I didn't like having to gaze up at him, yet I always enjoyed seeing him when he was sent to our door.

"*Bonsoir*, Philippe," I said.

The sound of scampering dogs coming to explore made me step out into the hallway and shut the door quickly behind me. I crossed my arms over my chest, embarrassed to be seen in my nightdress. "What is it?"

"I slipped free from my duties," Philippe said, a flush rising to his face. "I wanted you to be the first to hear the news."

My mind was tired of news. Though I had been escorted several times by Philippe with Stabdille to visit Bretagne, the last time this page had brought news, it had been of the worst possible kind. The past month had left me as tired and vulnerable as an orphaned newborn puppy. "Please, only if it's good news."

"It is, I promise. Madame will be pleased. The war with Germany is to end this very month."

"How do you know this?"

"A page has ears—that's all I can say."

"Oh, this is good news." Madame had written of entire German villages that had been burned by the French. "She will be quite happy to hear it, though I'm sure she will already know this. Certainly the king will tell her before I do. Still, thank you. This is a great kindness—the best kind of news."

"And there's more," he continued. "Already

Marie-Adélaïde and the king are making plans to have a grand Christmas ball to celebrate the coming peace. It's to be a celebration for the whole court."

"You have very good ears," I said.

He pulled his earlobes. "Like a rabbit's," he said with a smile. Then he looked at me intently. "I also have good eyes. I can see you're the prettiest girl at court."

I turned away, awkward as a parrot off its perch. No one had ever told me I was pretty, not even my father, who saved his compliments for my spelling, reading, and questioning skills. A strange warmth rose from my neck to my face.

"I must go," I said, pivoting in my wool stockings and grabbing the door handle. Instead of finding the handle, I walked into the edge of the door. I flushed again, this time with embarrassment.

"You'll be at the Grand Ball, then?" Philippe asked.

"Maybe," I said with a shrug. I stepped back into Madame's apartment, closed the door, and flopped back on the sofa.

Stabdille jumped in my lap, his wet nose to my face, as if to ask, "What's wrong with you?"

13 *Royal Sled Race*

The whole palace buzzed with preparations for
the coming ball. Women talked of nothing but new
dresses, the finest fabrics, and seamstresses and tailors.
"If only money were not so scarce," I often heard, but
that didn't stop Marie-Adélaïde's plans for the Grand
Ball from proceeding. The king declared that everyone, even the court servants, was to be in a new outfit
for the celebration.

"A dress of powder blue," Madame said to the
seamstress who measured my outstretched arms.
"Simple," she said, "but graceful enough to bring a
smile back to Cécile's face." It was true. Despite
Madame's efforts, I had smiled little during the past
month.

In the midst of my grief, all the talk of the ball

annoyed me. I was relieved, then, when the talk
turned to something else: sled races. A few days before
Christmas, the king declared the ice safe for skating
and racing. In the afternoon sunshine, I walked the
dogs to the canal to watch Bretagne race.

Six sleds waited at the starting ribbon, each
harnessed to a splendid pony, and each pony held
by an attending groom.

Bretagne sat in a carved wooden sled with wooden
runners, with his little brother, Anjou, squarely on
his lap. Anjou sat still, pointing at the pony ahead
of them. "Po-ny," he said.

"That's right," Bretagne said. "That's a pony."

Nearby, their elderly governess, Madame de
Ventadour, waited, her hands nestled in a muff, her

nose red from the freezing air. "Just a moment more," she said, "and then Anjou will have to get out. The race is nearly ready to begin."

I had never dreamed of such sleds. One sled's bow was carved into a gold angel; another sled was shaped like a seashell with a woman's head at its bow. Bretagne's sled was the most beautiful. The young prince sat on a blue velvet seat atop a huge carved turtle. His sled hinted at slowness, but I hoped he would win. For this race, all riders were descendants of the king. The king, I had learned, had fathered many children in his earlier years, and not all by his first and second wives.

A hush fell.

Marie-Adélaïde, pretty as a portrait in a red and white cloak, announced, "The race will mark the beginning of the court's Christmas festivities!"

A soldier stood to one side of the racers, who were lined up at the ribbon laid across the snow.

I kept an eye out for Philippe. He had become my favorite page at court, though, of course, I would not tell him that.

"I shall win the race, you'll see!" Bretagne shouted to Stabdille and me. "I am the king's great-grandson. Nothing shall stop me from winning!"

"Except excessive pride, perhaps," his governess whispered to me.

I smiled, understanding well that this was a private joke.

Madame de Ventadour stepped to the sled and put her arms out to Anjou, who was nearly two years old now. He shook his head at her. "Non," he said, then babbled something more in protest.

"Come, Anjou. You've had your chance to sit with Bretagne. Now it's nearly time for the race to begin." She scooped the toddler into her arms, her back arching at his weight.

Stabdille began to bark at the ponies, as if it were his job to tell them how to pull the sleds. I knelt beside him, the snow up to the ankles of my boots. "Shush," I said. "You can't go with them." I stroked the dog's back and felt his little body quivering beneath my hand.

Sun glinted off the fresh snow, casting more

diamonds about than even King Louis could accumulate in his lifetime. Diamonds were strange. In my mind, they were just sparkling little stones. I had noticed that Marie-Adélaïde wore diamonds only in the king's presence, but when she was away from his side, she dressed more comfortably than the other women at court. She wore loose dresses and almost no jewelry, and she spent little time styling her hair. I wondered about my mother. Had she been anything like the princess? I longed to know who she was before she was forced to settle in Rileaux after my father's banishment. Like the nearby statue of a centaur—man from the waist up and horse from the waist down—I felt my life caught between two worlds. I was neither peasant nor nobility.

A gunshot startled me from my thoughts. The ponies bolted forward, the crowd cheered, and Stabdille pulled at his leash as hard as he could to follow, though I held him firmly. Snow rose in small clouds behind each sled, and I clapped my mittens together. "Go, Bretagne!" I shouted. I had come to enjoy the boy and truly wished him well, so my cheers were genuine. But then a thought struck me. As I looked around at all the courtiers, noses red from standing in the cold, shoulders caped, and hands in muffs and mittens, I realized that we were all a ready and constant audience for the royal family. The royals needed us as much as we needed them.

I cheered again, half of me happy for Bretagne, the other half of me wishing I could race down the canal in a sled myself. In Rileaux, no one had cared if I ran through the snow, skidded across ice, or threw snow-balls. I missed Papa and I missed my freedom, both of which I had always taken for granted.

The sleds turned at the end of the canal and headed back. Ponies galloped through snow toward the finish line and the cheering crowd. Trumpets sounded. I could no longer muster up much enthusiasm. My grief weighed me down again. I was grateful for the food and shelter I had, yet I felt myself growing more invisible with every day, more distant from my true self.

Just then, a moan went up from the crowd. I focused on the sleds that were racing across the finish. Just behind the line, a rider was lying facedown in the snow. The pony stopped, waiting for someone to right its toppled and now-empty turtle sled.

My heart lurched.

"Bretagne!" I called, and dashed with the dogs after Madame de Ventadour to the young boy's side. With the leashed dogs pulling in every direction, I fell several steps behind as Madame de Ventadour rushed to Bretagne and gathered him up in her sturdy arms. "Are you all right?" she asked.

"Put me down!" he ordered, a smile spreading across his face. He wiped snow from his brocade jacket and his round face. "That was fun!"

Just as I neared him, I was brought short by a strong hand on my shoulder, then dragged backward, away from the toppled turtle and its rider. The dogs began barking, tangling and tumbling on their leashes through the snow after me.

I spun around, angry that someone would treat me so roughly.

A soldier glared down at me, his nose out-distancing his chin.

"You are not a servant of the Bourgogne family!"

"I'm a friend! I only wanted to make sure he was not hurt."

"My job is to guard the young boy. I don't care about your intentions. You may be carrying a dagger, for all I know."

I looked around for a familiar face. Where were Françoise and Madame, who had said they would watch the races? I searched for their faces in the throng.

"Just ask the princess, Marie-Adélaïde," I pleaded. "She'll tell you." I felt the ground slipping out from beneath me. How was I to have known that I wasn't allowed to comfort Bretagne? I despised this world filled with its invisible rules.

"There! She's with her son now. You can ask her."

With the commotion, the dogs barked more loudly, yipping at a high pitch.

"I remember you—at the fountain," the soldier continued. "Clearly, you still don't know your place, Mademoiselle." And with that, he ordered me to follow.

14 *The Grand Ball*

Later that afternoon, after Madame was summoned to explain my behavior to a senior officer,
I returned—head down—with the dogs to Madame's
apartment. Because I had dashed from the crowd
toward Bretagne, a royal family member, I would
not be able to attend the Grand Ball.

I sat on a cushion and brushed Stabdille, feeling
as lowly and vulnerable as a snail without its shell.

Madame looked up from her solo card game.
"I know that the rules of court are not easy to follow,
Cécile, especially for someone who has grown up
away from here. But you must be extra mindful of
your actions." She paused, as if considering whether
or not to speak further. "Just after the race, when I
protested to Madame de Maintenon about your

treatment, she told me that the day you arrived, she had instructed her guards to keep a careful eye on you because of your background and," Madame added, "especially since you're here in my household." Madame huffed and snapped a card down on her table. "So much for our coming Grand Peace with Germany—that old hag."

"I'll try, Madame. Above all, I don't want to cause trouble for you."

"Don't worry about me, Cécile. You just do your best and try not to draw undue attention to yourself."

I bowed my head. "Oui, Madame."

Stabdille licked my hand, as if to reassure me. I hugged him close, then brushed his tail. I vowed once again to learn my place, lest I dishonor

Madame and find myself with nowhere to go. I
remembered the woman pleading for bread, and
Madame's letters filled with stories of food shortages
in Paris. I was an orphan now. If I were to lose my
position, I might starve. I could no longer risk
childish behavior.

I stole a glance at my new blue dress, gathered at
the sleeves and waist, but then I looked away. The
seamstress had delivered it while I was being treated
like a criminal. What did I care about a new dress
and going to the Grand Ball, anyway? Why should
I care about the goings-on at the palace when I
continued to be treated with suspicion? I wanted
to huff the way Madame did and call Madame de
Maintenon names, but I guarded my tongue.

With great difficulty, I tried not to look at the
dress for the rest of the afternoon, not to stare at its
ruffles and delicate stitching. I didn't want to care
about anything at court. But I did. I would have
enjoyed wearing the dress and seeing Philippe.

The special evening mass lasted an eternity, and the congregation was restless, unable to sit or stand still because of the Grand Ball following the service. The priest spoke longer than ever, trying to prepare the souls of his flock before they embarked on a night of dancing and merrymaking.

When mass finished, I walked the dogs back to Madame's apartment, glad for at least their company. In the nearly empty hallways, I peered out through windows as fireworks filled the night sky. Streams of white and gold and blue shot like a thousand stars over the crowd huddled below. I hurried on, not wanting to be punished for stopping in the hall to watch the display. I glanced around to see if anyone was approaching; then, in frustration, I huffed out loud. It was of little consolation.

That evening, the sounds of music and laughter filtered through the double doors to where I lay on my bed beneath my goose-down quilt, fully dressed in my new light blue gown, with the dogs cuddled around me.

"Stabdille," I said, "if I could, I would turn you

into a prince and we'd dance together . . . just like *Cendrillon*." I sat up and pretended to wave a wand like the one that Marie-Adélaïde carried at ceremonies. Stabdille followed my hand and imaginary wand with a twisting and turning of his head. I laughed.

"There," I said. "My request is granted. You are a handsome prince."

I stood up, gathered Stabdille in my arms, his little head resting on my shoulder, and we twirled around the candlelit room. "My, but you dance divinely!"

A familiar scratching came at the door.

My heart jumped. This time, I knew it was Philippe. I recognized his scratch—not too hard and not too soft.

When I opened the door, I couldn't hold back my smile. "Merry Christmas, Philippe," I said, for I knew it was past midnight.

"Merry Christmas," he said, bowing so low that I thought he might topple over. Then he stood upright, straightening his vest of dark blue velvet. "I come with a request from young Bretagne," he said. "He wants you to come to the ball. Actually, he wants to dance with you at the ball."

I felt myself almost float in the air. "Dance with me?" I laughed. "Bretagne?"

"I overheard, and he says he won't go to bed until—"

"Yes, that's Bretagne," I said. "But, how can I? My punishment. I was commanded not to attend the ball."

"The king overruled," Philippe said. "I watched Bretagne go directly to the top. Besides, this evening, I think the king would grant any milkmaid's request. Even Madame de Maintenon is smiling."

"Truly a Christmas miracle," I said wryly.

I glanced at the closed door behind me. "I can't risk leaving the dogs behind." So I leashed them all and nearly skipped down the hall alongside Philippe.

"Your dress," said Philippe, glancing out of the corner of his eye, "is lovely, but not nearly as pretty as you."

Heat rose again to my face, along with a smile. "Philippe," I said teasingly, "I think you've been here too long. You're almost sounding like a courtier."

"With one exception," he said.

"What's that?"

"I may be the only honest one here."

At the ball, the room sparkled with people in jewel-studded white wigs and colorful dresses and waistcoats. And although they were dressed far more simply than nobles, even the servants wore new clothes. Philippe led me toward the young royal family and the king, who was in earnest conversation with Madame de Maintenon. Nearby, under the gaze of their governess, Bretagne and little Anjou lay belly-down on large velvet cushions. Despite the late hour, even they were at the celebration and not asleep in the royal nursery.

"Cee-cee!" Anjou cried. He darted between the dogs and wrapped his arms around my legs, nearly tripping me. My visits to see Bretagne had not gone unnoticed by his little brother.

"Hello, Anjou," I said, curtsying, just to be safe. Toddler or not, he was one of the royal family.

Then Bretagne rose from his cushion, his sweet

young face absolutely beaming. "Let's dance," he said, stretching out both hands to mine.

"Excuse me," called Madame from a nearby chair. "Cécile, you cannot dance with royalty," she began seriously, then broke into a smile as she undid the pearls around her neck, "without the proper accessories." She motioned for me to step closer, then fastened her strands of pearls around my neck and her bracelets on my wrists. To finish off my appearance, she handed me her white ostrich-feather fan.

"Oh, Madame!" I said, unable to hold back my delight.

"For the dance only," Madame said.

I nodded. "Merci." I understood my position as a servant and appreciated Madame's generosity. She showed me as much love as she could within the confines of her royal position.

I studied the dancers, who were turning with precision across the parquet floor, and hoped I wasn't expected to join the minuet. I had no idea how to dance it. I reached down, my hands twice the size of Bretagne's. Towering over him, I followed his wandering and circling lead at the edge of the ball-room floor. Each time I turned a circle, I smiled back at Philippe, who held the dogs for me.

When Bretagne finally stopped and bowed to me, I curtsied in return. "Thank you, Bretagne, for this dance."

"Thank you, Cee-cee," he said with a laugh. "That's a good nickname for you."

I noticed that Marie-Adélaïde and her husband, seated near the king, were watching us. The princess motioned for me to come closer. I prayed that I hadn't done something wrong this time.

I curtsied before her. "Yes, *Dauphine* Marie-Adélaïde?" I hoped I had her title right.

"My sons adore you," she said. "They have a host of nursemaids and their governess, yet they both asked to see you this evening. Such a compliment."

I wondered if I was dreaming. This surely was turning out to be the kind of evening found only in stories. "Thank you," I said.

I was about to tell her how much I enjoyed her sons when the princess winced. Her forehead creased with pain. She grabbed her jaw with one hand and covered her eyes with the back of her other hand.

"Oh no!" I said. Had someone poisoned her? I began to scan my memories for anything my father might have done to treat poisoning. "Shall I send someone to fetch a doctor, Your Highness?"

Bourgogne clasped his wife's shoulder and looked up at me with calm and steady eyes. "My dear wife can take part in only some of tonight's joy. Since she came to court—at just about your age—her teeth have caused her constant pain. And yet she is always generous to others. She recently cooked a dinner all by herself, for the king."

I nodded, but inside I laughed a bit. I had managed, countless times, to prepare meals for my father without the help of servants.

"And," he continued, "she planned tonight's grand celebration to lift everyone's spirits here at court." He kissed her cheek. "You, my dear, are not only my love, but the inspiration for all of France."

"I'm sorry for your pain, Dauphine," I said to Marie-Adélaïde. "I hope to help bring you only joy."

She uncovered her eyes and removed her hand from her jaw, which was slightly swollen. She nodded at me, her eyes filled with both pain and affection.

I curtsied deeply and, although I didn't want to leave the festivities, I turned to go. Reluctantly, I returned Madame's jewels and fan with a curtsy and a thank you. Then, holding my head high, I took the leashes and dogs from Philippe, who happily escorted me back to the apartment.

That evening, before I fell asleep, I thought about Philippe—and about Marie-Adélaïde. I was grateful to Philippe for his friendship and to the Dauphine for her kindness. I wished to be more like her. Despite her constant pain, she seemed to live with joy and inner strength. Already I had lived long enough to know that life was not filled with much joy. Already I had felt the crushing loss of both my mother and my father. And yet, like the flowing Seine River, life carried me forward. I had no idea what the future held for me, but whatever it might be, I was determined to do my best. I would be strong and spirited and dutiful, and I would serve the future queen with as much love and loyalty as possible.

In the wee hours of that Christmas morning, nothing could possibly have dampened my mood. The long war with Germany was going to end soon, and the coming peace brought hopes of easing the hardships of the people. And despite my mistakes, I had found favor with not only Madame and Philippe but also—to my utter amazement—the future king and queen of France and their children. Like arriving at a lovely and unexpected bend in the river, I could have drifted in that moment forever.

15 Marly

Because I was a servant to Madame's dogs, most people paid little attention to me, and I often overheard conversations that many at court would never hear. This was especially true one January evening at the Marly hunting estate, when I stood against the wall, along with several other servants. An outbreak of measles had struck Versailles, and the prince and princess's household and servants had been hit especially hard. Already, two hundred people had been carried away for burial. Françoise was beside herself with worry, as her favorite suitor was a merchant who sold to the royal Bourgogne family. Out of fear of contagion, the royal family had left the palace for Marly. Of course, wherever they went, we went.

That evening, the royal family gathered before the marble hearth. A fire roared like a dragon with an unquenchable appetite, kept satisfied by a crippled servant who continually fed it logs. At my back, the wall iced my shoulders. I wanted to lie by the warmth of the fire and sleep, but I stood dutifully, watching the dogs and trying to stay awake.

Madame reclined on a couch-like *chaise longue*, her dogs curled on her outstretched skirts, except for Stabdille, who lay on his back on a rug, paws toward the flickering candelabra. After playing for an hour with the boys, he was exhausted. The king chatted with Bretagne and Anjou, who took turns sitting in their great-grandfather's lap as he told them stories about his early days as a soldier. I stifled my yawns and pinched myself, desperately trying to keep my eyes open.

The young royal couple leaned back on cushions. "I'm serious, *chéri*," Marie-Adélaïde said to Bourgogne. "Who will you marry when I'm gone?"

That night, caught in the amber glow of firelight, with her head and sore jaw wrapped in white cloth, the princess looked almost like a nun.

"Should that ever happen, my love," her husband answered, "I'd never remarry. In a week I'd follow you to the grave."

On the far side of the room stood Philippe, who served the Bourgogne household. At the conversation, his eyes met mine. I tried not to smile but felt a familiar warmth rise to my cheeks. He had taken to teasing me about it, calling me his "rosebud friend." I bit the insides of my cheeks to compose myself. In such a gathering, a good servant should be about as noticeable as a plain chair.

The conversation continued. Marie-Adélaïde shook her head. "But I'm already twenty-five years old. With each year, that prediction by the Turin astrologer haunts me more than ever. What if it's true, that this year I—"

"Enough talk. I can't imagine that your life could possibly end before you reach twenty-seven. I highly doubt God would have directed your steps to Versailles if He had such plans. More than ever, France needs you." He kissed her cheek. "And I need you."

Their talk turned to politics, but my mind churned their words round and round as I thought more about the strange prediction by an astrologer from Turin, Italy. From my father, who had called such things "sheer folly," I had learned not to take such predictions seriously. "Far better to think with the minds God gave us," he would say. And yet, I felt some fear, and I hoped that the prediction about Marie-Adélaïde would not come true. I resolved to observe her more closely from then on. When I glanced at Philippe again, his eyes were downcast. He was perhaps pondering the same thoughts.

We went back to Versailles during the first week of
February. I was in Marie-Adélaïde's apartment showing Anjou and Bretagne the new tricks Stabdille had
learned. With small pieces of bread that I had saved
from my meals, I had taught him to roll over, to sit
on his hind legs with his front feet in the air, and to
shake his head back and forth. The boys laughed
and took turns rewarding Stabdille for his genius.

Often while we played, visitors came and went
from Marie-Adélaïde's quarters. But that noon, a
courtier old enough to be the princess's father
tapped me on the shoulder while the princess was
in conversation. In his outstretched hand was an
exquisite silver snuffbox. "Please give this to Marie-
Adélaïde," he told me. "Tell her it is the finest
Spanish snuff, a gift from the Duc de Noailles."

I glanced around the room. The other servants
were busy, so I did as asked. "Oui, Monsieur," I said.

As soon as Marie-Adélaïde was free, I left the boys
with Stabdille and stepped to her chair with a curtsy.

"Yes, Cécile? What is this lovely gift from an even
lovelier girl?"

I held out the round silver box, engraved with a cherub and flowers. As requested, I told her whom the gift was from and that it was, as he had said, "the finest Spanish snuff."

"I love gifts," she said, her smile as bright as the sun glinting off another snowfall. With delicate hands, she opened the silver box. She licked the tip of her forefinger, dipped it in the dark powder, brought the snuff to her nostril, and inhaled deeply. She smiled. "Yes, it's quite good indeed." She rose and set the snuffbox on her dressing table.

I curtsied again and returned to the boys and to Stabdille, who was now busy chasing a ball of yarn across the room. Shortly after, Stabdille and I returned to the apartments, where I spent the afternoon reading Madame's letters.

That evening, the hour was late when Madame climbed into her canopied bed, and the dogs rushed to their spots on the blanket. "Have you heard the news, Cécile?" she asked. "Marie-Adélaïde has fallen terribly ill."

My stomach twisted as I remembered the snuffbox.

What if it had contained poison? I was the one who had given it to her!

Madame turned on her side and continued. "Some say she ate too much rich food. She had served a fine little cake she herself had made for dinner. Lots of white cheese, sugar, and maize flour—I had asked about the ingredients. And within the hour, she began to shiver with fever and felt pain again in her lower cheek."

I drew a breath. Her jaw. That was it. It wasn't poison, as I had so quickly feared.

"She couldn't even go to visit the king as usual after supper. For the first time, she refused. Already the doctors have given her gouttes d'Angleterre and opium, and they've bled her twice, but nothing, it seems, is easing her pain or fever. She asked one of her ladies to get her new little snuffbox, but they could not find it."

"It's on her table," I said. "I saw her put it there."

"Well, it's apparently not there now. Not a trace of it to be found. Of course, the doctors suspect poisoning."

That night I tossed beneath my down quilt. I
worried about Marie-Adélaïde and tried not to let
my mind repeat the conversation I had so recently
heard at Marly between her and her husband. I con-
sidered every movement, every word of the Duc de
Noailles and whether I had seen a flicker of malice
in his face, or a shifting of his eyes, but I couldn't
remember any such thing. I had simply taken the
snuffbox from his hands, as requested, and delivered
it to the princess. Marie-Adélaïde was my future
queen, whom I had vowed to serve to the best of
my ability. God knew I had not intended her any
wrong. But where was the snuffbox? Who would
have dared remove it from her room? Questions
and predictions plagued me, and as the black night
turned to gray shadows outside the windows, I
prayed for her health and well-being and for that
of France. Eventually, I prayed myself to sleep.

16 *Nightfall at Versailles*

Four days later, as we walked to mass, Françoise and Madame were talking. I trailed two steps behind them, listening.

"They have found red marks on her skin," whispered Madame.

"No!" Françoise stopped in the hall, sunlight highlighting her creamy skin and chestnut hair. "Measles, then?"

Madame nodded. "That's what the doctors say. You know well how I once despised her, how as a spoiled child she tormented me to no end, pulling dishes of food right out from under my nose—"

I waited. I could barely imagine that Marie-Adélaïde could have behaved so rudely. It seemed completely beyond her character. Whatever she had

been like as a child, spoiled as she might have been, she had left the worst of herself in the past.

"But of late," Madame continued, her voice softening, "we had made amends, and I do not wish any harm to come to her."

My heart quickened, and I made the sign of the cross over my chest. Not everyone died of measles. Marie-Adélaïde was strong in spirit and body, except for her constant jaw and tooth pain. She certainly would survive.

But I was wrong. Only two days later, the Turinese prediction began to come true. From Madame's letters, I learned every detail. When Marie-Adélaïde's fever continued, the doctors had bled her several times and had given her My Lady Kent powder, which caused her to sweat profusely and break out into an "angry red rash." Then she was placed into a warm bath. Finally, the priest gave her the last rites, and the doctors bled the poor princess again, this time from her foot.

I read Madame's letters and wept.

With all hope gone, ordinary people were allowed to press past the guards and to crowd into Marie-Adélaïde's apartment. I longed to return to the days when I had joined the princess and her ladies, bring-ing Stabdille to play with Bretagne and little Anjou. Now, amid the crowd, I stood with everyone else behind the banister that divided the public from her canopied bed. I stood in the queen's ornately decorated apartments, where, as future queen, Marie-Adélaïde had already given birth to her children in public. Now she was suffering and dying in public. I could not imagine what it was like to be her, to live where everyone gazed upon you in your most private and painful moments.

Three doctors surrounded her bed, its canopy nearly reaching the tall ceiling. Dr. Fagon paced.

Had my father been there, he would have refused to allow the princess to be bled so many times. She might have been sitting up in bed, sipping teas and returning to her buoyant self. But now—my mind and stomach turned at what I was seeing—now she hovered on the edge of death's black chasm.

A hush fell across the crowd, with murmurs of "Quiet! Silence! The princess is speaking!"

Ever so faintly, like a ribbon carried on a soft breeze, her words drifted. "To-day . . . a princess," she said, her voice raspy, "to-morrow . . . nothing."

Grief tightened my throat. If only she were joking, as she so often did, trying to make light of a difficult situation and getting the court to laugh. It would be like her to just sit up and say, "There! A perfect joke!" But she did not. Courtiers and common people dabbed at their eyes. Chins quivered. The room was eerily silent.

I could not stay until the end. Françoise had allowed me to leave the dogs in her care, but not for long. She, too, wanted to be at the princess's side. Tears flowed down my face as I pushed through the dense crowd and returned to the apartment. I lay on my bed and wrapped my arms around myself.

That night, word spread throughout the palace. Marie-Adélaïde had died at 8:30 that evening. With the news, Madame received word to ready herself to go to Marly to avoid contagion. I gathered the dogs and prepared to leave.

In the courtyard, under a still and starless sky, the dogs surrounded my skirts in a semicircle. I waited beside Françoise and Madame for the coach. We watched the king, who was at the front of the procession, as he climbed heavily into his coach with Madame de Maintenon.

"The king needs to be alone with his grief," Madame said, her voice wavering. "Never has anyone brought him so much joy and warmth. He and the princess shared games of pall-mall, masked balls, and drives together after deer. She was everything to him."

Madame touched a handkerchief to her eyes and nose. "I cannot bear to see him like this. His grief would melt a heart of stone." Then she began to sob silently, hunched forward, her back rising and falling. I risked overstepping my place and pressed my face to her cloaked back.

After a few moments, she stood tall again and faced me. "And you remind me so much of her."

"I do?"

She nodded. "You have the same spring in your step, the same dancing in your eyes. Imagine," she said, glancing around the courtyard as if she were looking into the past, "she was only your age— twelve—when she came here amid great fanfare, with the hopes of many countries resting on her future role as queen of France. And at fourteen, she married." She shook her head. "Life is so short . . . so very, very short. I will never understand."

"Nor will I," Françoise added, her white makeup streaked from crying.

Madame continued, choosing to be strong for all of us, it seemed. "God gives and He takes. In the middle of it all, I try to trust that some good will come of our disaster, impossible as it seems."

Our coach, led by eight horses, clattered toward us.

I still could not grasp that Marie-Adélaïde was gone. Sorrow drenched me like a cold rain. Then I realized that I hadn't seen her husband the Duc de Bourgogne at her bedside. Certainly he should have been present at her death. If ever a man loved a woman, the prince had loved his wife. But he had been absent all evening. "Where is the prince?" I asked.

"He was sent to Marly a few days ago. The doctors forced him to stay away for fear of contagion. He must be beside himself with grief. I fear he will take this loss badly."

The coach stopped and the driver stepped down, opening the door for Madame.

I shuddered, suddenly remembering the prince's words beside the fire. If Marie-Adélaïde died, he had said, in a week he would follow her to the grave. I did not need to remind Madame of his words, for indeed she must have heard them as well. Some things were better left unspoken.

In the week that followed, events unrolled like an endless carpet. Madame was so beside herself with grief that she could not even speak to me. Indeed, I rarely saw her, as she kept nearly continual company with the king and Madame de Maintenon. And so, as was my duty, I read the letters Madame wrote. I looked for spelling errors and, mostly, I read and reread the letters for their meaning, trying to understand the events that had happened—an effort as impossible as my becoming a princess.

14 February 1712
. . . I am convinced that the doctors have killed this poor princess. . . Now it is all over. I cannot look at the King without getting tears in my eyes . . .

Madame's letters reported the events to her family and to friends across Europe. I didn't want to believe her words could be true. Was it possible that Marie-Adélaïde had died at the hands of the court doctors? If they had left her alone, would she still be alive? I wished my father had been there. He would have stood up to the court doctors.

Stabdille stood with his nose to the door, whining. I leashed the dogs, and took them outside to the courtyard, where I drew deep breaths of much-needed crisp air.

To my dismay, the news in Madame's letters over the next few days only turned worse.

18 February 1712

I had thought today I would only have to write about the sad ceremony in which I had to participate at Versailles yesterday, but a new disaster has befallen us, for the good Monsieur le Dauphin [the prince] has followed his wife and died this morning at nine o'clock. You can easily imagine the dreadful sadness that this loss has brought to all of us. The King's grief is so great that I tremble for His Majesty's health. It is a horrible loss for the entire kingdom, for Monsieur le Dauphin was a virtuous and just lord, and sensible too; France could not suffer a greater loss, and everyone here will be the poorer for it; I am moved to the depth of my soul . . . he relieved the King of as many

*burdens as he could, was charitable, and gave alms
liberally; in fact he sold all of his late mother's jewels
and gave the money to impoverished wounded officers.
He did as much good as was in his power and has
never harmed anyone. I do not think that what we
shall see here has ever happened before, namely that
a husband and wife are taken to Saint-Denis in the
same hearse. I am still in such a shock that I cannot
seem to recover. The sadness here is indescribable, it
fairly looks as if all of us here will die one by one.*

Poor Madame. I knew there was little I could do
to ease her pain. I perfumed the dogs, played ball
with them during the day, and did everything I
could to make them tired and content, ready to
snuggle with Madame and give her some small
comfort when she retired for the night.

17 *Rumors of Poison*

Early the next morning, during the time of the king's council meeting, I recognized the scratch at the door—two short, one long—and smiled. In the midst of the court's gloomy mood, Philippe was the one person who eased mine. I set Madame's letter on her table, careful not to place it where the dogs might chew on it or trample it, and opened the door.

Philippe faced me, his expression sober. He opened his mouth but didn't speak. Finally he said, "Madame de Maintenon requests your presence."

"But . . . why? I can't imagine she wants to see Stabdille?"

"I don't know," he said with a shrug. "The doctors were entering her room as I left, and they didn't sound happy."

"But . . . the dogs. No one is here. I can't leave them."

"Then I advise that you bring them along. She is not a patient woman. I would not make her wait."

I leashed the dogs, who yawned and stretched, reluctant to leave their warm beds. Side by side, Philippe and I walked to Madame de Maintenon's apartment, situated between the king's apartments and the now empty queen's quarters. A heaviness settled in my chest as I passed Marie-Adélaïde's door, which I would never step through again. I would never again hear her laughter or hear her call me— *me*—by name. Again, I felt my eyes fill, but my hands held leashes, so I blinked back my tears. Philippe's pace was faster, more clipped than usual, and I hurried to keep up with him. Rarely did he walk ahead of me anymore. But something about this summons was different.

Philippe scratched on the door, and I entered the apartment. In a semicircle sat not only Madame de Maintenon but also the king and Madame herself, who barely met my eyes. What was this?

To the sides of their chairs stood three doctors: Dr. Fagon, the Head Physician; wild-eyed Dr. Boudin, who had been the princess's doctor and who kept running his hand over the top of his wig; and Dr. Maréchal, his arms crossed firmly over his paunchy middle.

Dr. Fagon stepped toward me. "Cécile Revel," he said slowly, emphasizing my last name.

In response, I curtsied as best I could with the dogs in tow. I swallowed so hard, I was certain that everyone in the room had heard.

"Where were you on the morning of February 5th?" he asked accusingly.

"I do not remember," I said, for honestly, I rarely paid close attention to the date, except when I read it in Madame's letters.

"Let me refresh your memory, then," he said, pacing back and forth before me. "You were in Marie-Adélaïde's apartment with her boys when the Duc de Noailles paid her a visit, isn't this true?"

"Yes, I was there when he visited, but I do not remember the date."

"And what do you remember of a silver snuffbox?"

I glanced at Madame, hoping for some idea of where this conversation was leading, but her gaze was on the dogs, clearly avoiding my eyes. I felt abandoned.

"I remember it had a cherub on it, beautifully carved . . ."

"You were close enough to see such details?"

"Oui, Monsieur. I was asked to give it to the princess, which I did. She had been busy talking with another courtier."

"So you held it, then . . . in your very own hands?"

I nodded.

Dr. Fagon circled closer, his voice dropping to a near whisper. "And did you happen to add poison to the snuffbox before you gave it to Marie-Adélaïde?"

"No!" I said. "I would never—"

He held up his hand. "Of course not. But the facts are that you were in the room, your hands were on the snuffbox, and you spoke with the very man who delivered it. Isn't this true?"

"Yes, but—" Beneath my dress, my legs trembled violently. Sweat dripped in a steady line down my back.

Madame opened her mouth as if to speak up, but then closed it again. For a brief moment, she glanced at me. I saw nothing in her expression that told me she believed I was guilty. But standing there, I felt guilty, even though I knew I had done nothing wrong.

"Consider yourself under suspicion. Our autopsies give us reason to believe," he said, measuring out his words, "that poison was involved in our beloved prince and princess's deaths."

Standing off to the side, Dr. Boudin ran his hand again over his wig as he stepped forward. "Rumors of the worst possible kind warned before her death that there would be an attempt on her life, and that of the prince." He slashed the air with his arm. "And now, with no one finding the snuffbox, it can only mean one thing!"

"Wait, gentlemen," Dr. Maréchal said, not moving his folded hands from his belly. He stood planted as solid as a tree. "You all know as well as I do that there is no evidence of poisoning. Try as you might, you have to agree that as with all other cases of this measles outbreak, the rash and the symptoms have been the same."

"Huh!" exclaimed Dr. Boudin. "Then what about the shriveled hearts and organs, the strange condition of the blood?"

"A raging fever, gentlemen," Dr. Maréchal replied calmly, "so deep-seated that few signs of it appeared outwardly. A fever—sufficient in itself to have caused death."

Dr. Fagon's face turned red as a poppy. Finally, he shouted, "A fire that consumed the whole interior of their bodies—nothing short of a mild yet powerful poison! Dr. Boudin and I agree on this, and you dare to contradict us? We witnessed their excruciating deaths, as did you, and yet you will not stand with us in our findings of poisoning?"

Dr. Boudin's eyes grew wide. "The whole court is buzzing with 'poison, poison'! Someone who has eyes on the throne could be using this girl, who so quickly found her way into the favor and confidences of the princess. She may indeed be part of a larger, black-hearted plot."

"Lies!" Madame shouted, rising from her chair and nearly putting her face in the doctor's. "Cécile is not capable of such evil deeds!" The room was still for a moment, and then Madame backed away and sat back in her chair, hands gripping the arms.

Dr. Boudin adjusted his wig and smoothed the front of his coat, as if Madame had messed up his ruffles.

"Your Highness," Dr. Maréchal said, turning slowly from the other doctors to the king, whose head was bowed. "Rumors are rumors, we all know that."

Not until that moment did I realize that the king was weeping, something he never would have done in public. Even in his sorrow, he had maintained all court council meetings and ceremonies.

"But Sire, to state that we have findings, well . . . I would hardly call them that. With these accusations of poisoning, we cause you more pain. Forgive us, Your Highness. Forgive us for fighting in your presence. I am of the professional opinion that these deaths are by a natural infection. I implore you, for the sake of your health and peace of mind, to put away dreadful fancies that, in my view, are wholly without substance."

The king, eyes puffy and cheeks streaked, looked first to his doctors, then to Madame de Maintenon, fingering her rosary beads and crucifix, and finally to Madame. Last, he looked at me, standing with the dogs, almost as if seeing me in the room for the first time, or ever. He half-smiled at me. "She was about your age when she came to court, did you know that?"

I nodded. "Yes, Your Highness."

"Are you capable of having poisoned your beloved princess?"

Tears welled in my eyes and his image blurred. I

shook my head fiercely. I couldn't say a word.

"Of course not," he said, his voice missing the notes of his usual stately tone. Then he turned to Dr. Fagon. "You are my good and faithful court doctor, but this time I am taking to heart the words of Dr. Maréchal. For the good of the throne, for the good of France, we will put this behind us." Then he lowered his head again.

"Cécile, that is all for now," Madame de Maintenon said. She waved to Philippe. "You may lead her back."

The whole walk back to the apartment, I was lost in my thoughts and did not say a word to Philippe. Watching Dr. Maréchal's bold actions in standing up to the other doctors and speaking his mind before the king, I felt as if I had been watching my own brave father. I longed to talk with Papa about all the events that had fallen like a black shroud on the court. He, more than anyone, would surely understand.

That evening, as I drifted to sleep on my bed, sounds filtered through the halls from the reopened gaming tables. But the laughter sounded false, the usual din flattened. At court, no one, from nobles to servants, could feign a true smile. Few cried openly, but from behind closed doors, wailing replaced the court's usual music. Even the fisherwomen from Paris, selling fish with shouts and gossip, had been unable to muster enthusiasm.

But in the midst of such sadness, I had brought half a smile to the king's face that day. That in itself was a miracle.

18 *No Safe Place*

The next day, Philippe was back at my door, this time sent by Madame de Ventadour, the young boys' governess.

Philippe's eyes and nose were red, surely from crying like everyone else at court. But his eyes brightened when he saw me step through the door.

"Rosebud," he said, startling me with a light kiss on my lips.

"Wh-what?" I stammered, completely taken by surprise. I didn't know if I should slap him or kiss him in return. For the hundredth time, heat shot up my neck to my cheeks. I glanced around, hoping no one had seen.

Then he returned to his duties as page. "The boys have returned from Meudon," he said, "where they

were kept from contagion. Bretagne is very sad and has requested that you pay a visit with Stabdille."

Madame rose with a *whoosh* of skirts from her chair and stood behind me, holding Stabdille in her arms. She kissed the top of his head, stroked his back, and said, "Of course you'll go with Cécile. I'll miss you, my little prince of a dog, but if anyone can help cheer the young princes now, it's you."

Then she set him on the ground before me. I found his leash, wrapped a shawl around my shoulders, for the halls were quite chilly, and set off with Philippe.

I was soon inside the nursery's grand rooms. On a miniature carousel, Bretagne rode a carved dolphin. Anjou was lying with his blanket on a sofa. They spotted us and came over, first hugging my legs and then hugging Stabdille, who wagged his tail in utter devotion.

"Bonjour, young prince," a courtier said from behind me. I turned to see another man in the doorway, standing next to Philippe. "Not prince—" he muttered, correcting himself. "I mean, Duc de Bretagne!"

"Please don't—" Bretagne said, reacting with a rush of tears at his new title. "It's too sad!" He spun away and ran back to the dolphin, which he hid behind as the carousel spun slowly.

"Too sad," Anjou mimicked, and ran back to his sofa.

One of the half-dozen nursemaids quickly closed the door behind us. "So thoughtless!" she said. "This court has no sense of what children need."

I had never seen the boys acting this shy before. I was unsure of what to do next.

Philippe stood by at the door. "Do you wish to return to your apartment?" he asked.

I shook my head, thinking. I remembered when I'd captured Madame's runaway horse, and the time

I'd left chunks of old cheese in the forest for a
rib-thin hound. This was the time to use the same
gentle approach with the boys. If anyone understood how painful it was to lose both a mother and
a father, it was I. The boys' feelings were as sensitive
as a fresh wound. If I tried too hard to help, they
would flee.

"Stabdille," I whispered, just loud enough for the
boys to hear, "let's make a nest by the windows."

Out of the corner of my eye, I saw Madame de
Ventadour lift her eyebrows.

Humming, I walked to the royal beds, both with
towering canopies and down comforters. "May I?"
I asked the governess, pointing to the goose-down
quilt on Bretagne's bed.

"Cécile, anything that will ease their sorrow. You
seem to know what you're doing." As I grabbed one
blanket, she grabbed another from Anjou's bed.
"Here, let me help."

Within seconds, I had piled one puffy blanket on
top of another, made an indentation in the middle,
just like a bird's nest, and then added pillows from

around the room, building the walls a bit higher. On a shelf, I found a gold-edged book of nursery rhymes, complete with pages of colorful pictures. I returned to my nest, where Stabdille had already settled himself, and lay back with my head against a pillow. The sun had already set beyond the tall window, edging dark clouds with fading gold.

As I expected, the boys didn't wait long to join me.

"What are you doing?" Bretagne asked. His voice was high, slightly irritated. "Don't you want to play with me?"

Beneath his sandy locks, his face was flushed.

"I thought you didn't want to see me, so I just decided to get comfortable over here." I patted the blankets. "There's room in our nest. Want to join us?"

He nearly threw himself into the pillows, facedown.

Immediately after, Anjou climbed over the pillows and plopped into my lap. "Cee-cee!" he said, wrapping his arms around my neck. It was then that I noticed that his face burned against mine. I didn't want to say anything, lest the magic spell of the moment be broken too quickly for the boys, but worry, like a stone, dropped into my heart.

"Are we birds, Cee-cee?" Anjou asked, whispering in my ear.

"Yes, we're good little birds."

"No, we're rabbits," Bretagne mumbled, his face still in the pillows. "Then no one can see us. We're underground. Safe in our den."

"Our soft, cozy, fur-lined den," I added.

"Mm-hmm," Bretagne replied, his back rising and falling slowly as he slipped quickly off to sleep. The poor little fellow, prince though he may be, was exhausted with sadness. God may have a divine plan for him, but he was still only a boy. I wondered whose job it had been to tell the boys that their mother and father had both died. I glanced at Madame de Ventadour, who sat in a chair, knitting, not far from us.

With Anjou in my lap, his head resting heavily against my chest, I turned the pages of the book as he fingered the images on paper. Stabdille rose, arched his back, and stretched. Then he settled himself between the boys, his front legs on Anjou's plump bare feet and his rear legs touching Bretagne's back.

Time stopped for our few moments together, and I loved those boys as if they were my own brothers. Bretagne began to mumble in his sleep.

"Maman . . . Papa . . ." he began, and the rest I couldn't understand. After a time, he flopped over, face up. And that's when I knew I had to speak up.

"Madame de Ventadour," I said, with a wave of my hand. "Please, come here."

She must have heard the worry in my voice. Despite her grandmotherly age, she nearly flew from her rocker and came to the side of our nest. I pointed at Bretagne's face, livid with red splotches.

"And Anjou is burning with fever, as well," I said, his head resting under my chin.

The governess examined him more closely. "The same rash," she said quietly. "God in heaven, help us. It is the same measles, I'm certain of it. I'm not sure that I want to, but I must notify the doctors."

She glanced around the room at the nursemaids, who had hovered closer, listening. A few had

already started to cry. Philippe stood at the door,
worry knotting his brow.

19 *When Sparrows Fall*

Within the hour, the king was alerted. Though the boys had been sprinkled with holy water at birth, they had not yet been baptized. A quick ceremony was arranged in the nursery.

"The king," the governess told me, "is as much concerned with the boys' spiritual fate as he is with their physical well-being."

The room filled with priests, doctors, the king, and Madame de Maintenon. The boys had grown so weak with fever that neither could stand on his own, so nursemaids held them in their arms for the ceremony.

The Bishop of Metz quoted scriptures reminding us that God has a plan. He knows the number of hairs on our heads and knows when every sparrow falls. I prayed that these two sparrows would not fall.

I could not bear the thought of it.

As the boys were baptized, a golden goblet of water was poured over their scalps and both were officially renamed "Louis," as Sons of the Blood of France. Then the bishop declared them baptized "in the name of the Father, Son, and Holy Ghost."

The moment the ceremony ended, the three court doctors, along with five others who had been called in from Paris, fell upon Bretagne and carried him to his bed. I watched it all from the edge of the room, not sure what I was supposed to do, other than hold onto Stabdille and wait to see if I was needed.

I cringed at seeing Bretagne in their care. If Dr. Maréchal had found no reason to suspect poison in the deaths of the princess and prince, then that left the real possibility that the doctors' methods had indeed contributed to their deaths.

From his bed, Bretagne cried out, "Please, don't bleed me!" I nearly ran to his side, but I held myself back. The doctors swarmed around his bed. I knew that if I tried to get close, an attending guard would only pull me away.

Metal sounded against metal as the doctors rummaged through their cases.

"There is no time to waste," Dr. Fagon declared. "We must proceed with every possible remedy!"

Voices murmured in agreement.

I hugged Stabdille in my arms for comfort, tears rolling steadily down my cheeks. Hovering near Madame de Ventadour's chair, where she held Anjou in her arms, I asked quietly, "Is there nothing we can do to stop them?"

A nursemaid drew close on the other side of the rocker. "Shall I place Anjou in his bed, so the doctors can care for him next, Madame?"

I couldn't hold my tongue. "No!" I whispered, the vehemence in my voice as strong as snake venom.

"They will kill him," I said, glancing across the room at Bretagne, stretched out so small in his huge bed. "Just as surely as they are killing his older brother now."

Madame de Ventadour lifted her hand. "Cécile," she whispered, "guard your tongue, lest you be punished . . . still, I fear your words are true." She motioned for all the nurses to gather closer. When they had formed a tight circle around her, she whispered, "Cécile is right. With all that has happened, we have no reason to believe the doctors will help—"

One nursemaid crossed her arms over her stout chest and glared at the governess. "Of course they will. The doctors know what they're doing—"

"Huh," said another, "just as they helped our beloved prince and princess?"

"They're busy now," Madame de Ventadour continued, "but soon enough they will turn to Anjou." She kissed the top of the two-year-old's head and looked up with dry eyes. "I swear I will not allow them to touch one so small. I don't care what happens to me. I will not allow it. Those of you who stand with Cécile and me, come. If you cannot, then remain here."

"Where will you go?" asked a nurse.

She motioned with her head to the small room next to the nursery, its door ajar. "We will lock ourselves in, if we need to."

Half the nursemaids chose to stay behind. Within moments, I joined the governess and three others. Once inside, I bolted the door to the white-tiled room that held a tub, a few chairs, a commode, and shelves of towels, bottles, and jars. I knew that by bolting the door, I was risking everything I had at court. I thought of Madame, who would be pained by my actions, and of Papa, who would be proud.

Madame de Ventadour carried Anjou, who opened his eyes halfway. He stretched an arm to me. "Cee-cee," he cried.

Madame de Ventadour motioned for me to sit down, which I did. She set little Anjou in my lap. As I held him, the nursemaids eased his heavy embroidered clothing from his body. In a silk sleep shirt, he lay his head on my shoulder, and like a flower dried up for lack of rain, he nearly wilted in my arms. I kissed the top of his head and forced back tears. "Be strong," I said. "Your friend Stabdille needs you to get well so you can play together soon."

Then Anjou's eyelids dropped and he drifted back to sleep.

Outside the door, voices of the remaining nurses turned to wailing. "Nooo!" one cried.

"Bretagne is dead!" cried another.

Hot tears rushed to my eyes. My heart shattered like glass. Never could I have had a worse nightmare. Not Bretagne, too!

The voices grew in volume, and above the din Dr. Fagon's voice boomed outside our bolted door. "Where is he?"

The outer room was suddenly silent.

"What's going on here?"

The door handle rattled, but the door held fast. "Anjou—is Anjou in there?" Dr. Fagon demanded.

"He is," Madame de Ventadour said, her voice unyielding. She clutched at the rosary beads around her neck, pressed the crucifix to her lips, and kissed it. "And the child," she said, "is receiving good care."

"By whom!?" Dr. Fagon demanded. "What is this nonsense? All the court doctors are here with me. I order you to open this door."

Deep voices murmured beyond the door. Again, the door handle rattled, this time harder.

"I will not," the governess said. "We will keep him warm and comfortable and you will not lay a finger on him, I swear it."

With each labored breath, Anjou's chest rose slowly against mine. So much had happened at court, and so much of it was tragedy that I had been powerless to stop. But I would not let them touch Anjou. They would have to tear him from my arms, for I would not give him up to the doctors' senseless treatment.

Pounding sounded on the door and arguments went back and forth between the court doctors. Dr. Maréchal argued with Dr. Fagon, saying, "Let this child be."

"Good governess," Dr. Fagon said, his voice softer

this time. "Open the door. The child must be bled, lest his fever consume him."

"Anjou is too small to be bled. You'll not do the same to him as—" She paused, her voice quieter. "Dr. Fagon . . . you must not touch this one."

"We'll have the guards force open the door."

"Dr. Fagon, this time, you must risk trying a different course of action."

The doctors must have taken up their posts outside our door. Through the night, Madame de Ventadour and her nurses took turns touching Anjou's forehead. "He's burning up," one said.

"I fear we will lose him, as well," said another.

"The same spots, dear God."

I knew that by holding Anjou, I could contract the same dreadful disease. I had suffered a mild case of measles as a young child, but not such a deadly form as this. I worried about Philippe, hoping he would survive contagion. But during those long, dim hours, my own welfare truly did not matter to me. I would do everything I could to help save Anjou, even if it was simply to hold him in my arms.

Indeed, if it were not too late already, I would have given my life to save dear Bretagne.

With Anjou's soft hair tucked under my chin, and with my arms wrapped around his waist, I held him—not too tightly, but firmly, for his limp body could easily slip to the floor, and I would not let that happen.

More than once, the nurses reached to take Anjou from my arms. Each time, he moaned in complaint, and so they let him be.

The hours ticked by slowly. But I remained awake, stroking Anjou's fine hair, lifting his chin when the nurses gave him water, and trying not to drown in a flood of sorrow.

20 *Sleeping Child*

All night long the candles burned, casting a soft glow across the room. As they burned low, day dawned gray through the window. Anjou's breathing had changed. It was no longer so labored. In my arms, he slept more calmly, his chest rising and falling rhythmically. Though his pudgy body was warm against mine, he felt cooler. I stroked his soft cheek with the back of my hand and peered sideways at his face. The spots that had been as bright as red paint had faded to smudges of pink.

Two of the nurses were asleep in chairs. Madame de Ventadour paced the room.

"Governess," I whispered. "The fever is gone."

She turned to me, her eyes shadowed with grief and worry. She stretched her wrinkled hand to

Anjou's forehead, rested it there for a long moment, then brought it to her own cheek. Her shoulders drooped with her heavy breath. "God be praised," she whispered. "God . . . be . . . praised."

I nodded. Two overwhelming feelings roosted like doves in my chest. One was a dark gray bird of sadness. The other was white and full of hope. I could not comprehend having lost the princess, the prince, and Bretagne in so short a time. That they were gone from my life did not seem possible. And yet, here was Anjou, who had survived the night— and was alive—sleeping soundly in my arms.

Madame de Ventadour leaned over me and kissed the top of my head. "You have your father's strength, Cécile," she whispered. "Thank you. I could not have taken this stand alone." Then she turned from me, gently woke her faithful nursemaids, and unbolted the door.

True to the king's policy, the court of Versailles

remained open to the public, even in the middle of such tragedy. But now the courtyard was draped in black, and the bodies of the prince and princess lay in the palace. For three days, anyone who wished to view them was allowed to do so.

Françoise watched the dogs so that I could walk past the open coffins. I stood in line for an endless time, determined I would make myself look when my turn came. As I neared, however, I felt numbed by the sounds of hammering, as carpenters constructed barriers to protect the coffins from the crush of so many people. I passed by, averting my eyes. I could scarcely breathe, partly from grief and partly from the great numbers of weeping spectators struggling to get closer.

At the end of those three days, a long procession assembled to escort the two large coffins—and one smaller one—to the cathedral of Saint-Denis in Paris.

Outside in the palace courtyard, amid the silent crowd, I waited beside Françoise. The night air was chilly. My breath formed white clouds, and the dogs huddled beneath my skirts. Madame's coach waited in line, with Madame seated inside, waiting, dreading—I knew—the endless hours of procession and funeral ceremony ahead.

French and Swiss guards filled the courtyard with a mournful, muffled drumbeat. A forest of white candles—carried by hundreds of footmen, soldiers, and guards on horseback—lit the night. For the last time, bishops and clergy sprinkled holy water on the coffins, while the priests of Versailles chanted the *Miserere* to mourn the dead.

All three coffins were placed in a towering coach that was draped in black and decorated with the wreathed coat of arms of France. Then the procession to Paris began. Wheels creaked, hooves and shoes clattered over stone, and not a word was spoken.

I could never have imagined such a tragic scene. My whole being felt as black as a dark night, lit only by the thoughts of having helped save young Anjou—frail and little as he was—France's remaining hope for a future king.

21 *Beyond Gilded Gates*

Sadness settled like a heavy fog over France, and yet daily life went on.

I tried to take comfort in routine. From dawn to dusk, I cared for Madame's dogs, read her letters, and looked forward to glimpses of Philippe and chance conversations with him. And every day a request came from Madame de Ventadour for me to bring Stabdille to visit Anjou. The prince was old enough to wonder where Bretagne and his father and mother had gone, but he was too young to understand that they were never coming back.

"Heaven," he said one day, after he had asked again about his maman. We were sitting in another nest we'd made together. "Me go heaven."

"No," I said, taking his pudgy dimpled hands in

mine. "You need to stay here, with me."

With each day that passed, I breathed easier, relieved that neither Philippe nor Madame de Ventadour nor I had contracted the disease. Still, I waited, wondering when I would be punished for my actions.

Nearly a month passed without incident when a different kind of scratch sounded at Madame's door. The hour was early. Madame's chambermaid had not yet added logs to the hearth's embers, and the curtains were still drawn. I scrambled from the warmth of my bed, opened the door, and peered out.

Two of the king's guards stood side by side. The one shaped like a barrel stepped forward, extending a scroll. "By orders of King Louis XIV," he began, "Cécile Revel is summoned to accompany us."

Madame shuffled up behind me. She rested her hand on my shoulder. "What nonsense is this?"

The guard handed her a letter. Madame broke the royal wax seal, opened the letter, and studied it, her chin trembling slightly.

I knew. Madame did not have to tell me what this

was about. For the past month, I had been waiting
for a summons. Again I would be called to stand
before the doctors and the king to explain my
behavior. I had defied the doctors' orders and stood
against them, and now that the court ceremonies
were over, justice would be served.

The guards grasped my upper arms.

I glanced at Madame. "Madame, where are they
taking me?" I asked.

She shook her head. "I don't know for certain,
Cécile, but I will find out. Let go of her," she told the
guards sternly. "Allow her to get dressed and at least
to say good-bye. I will be responsible for her."

I spun to Madame and hugged her tightly. She
bent toward me and whispered in my ear, "When
you fall from a horse, always remember to get back
on again—no matter how hard the fall."

I nodded, unable to speak. Then, with the door
half-closed, I quickly threw my green dress over my
nightgown and slipped on my shoes and cloak.

"I'll find out where you're going," Madame said.
"And I promise, I'll write."

I looked at her. "Thank you, Madame."

Then I kissed the dogs—one by one—who waited at her skirts. Finally, I picked up Stabdille and hugged him to my chest. Without him, I would never have come to be friends with the royal family. Without him, I would never have come to know Marie-Adélaïde and Bretagne, and I would never have been there to help save little Anjou. I pressed my wet face against Stabdille. "Be good," I whispered.

I did not want to make this harder, so I stepped out to the guards and, without looking back, silently allowed them to lead me away.

The guards walked me out of the palace through a side door.

"Where are you taking me?" I asked.

They did not answer, but kept their gaze fixed ahead.

Except for guards keeping watch, the courtyard was empty. A damp breeze swept across me, chilling me to my core. Despite the weather, birds sang from the groves and fields surrounding the palace. In the gray light of that April dawn, swallows darted

through the courtyard and pigeons pecked at the
damp cobblestone.

My legs felt stiff as logs. I did not want to leave
Madame and the dogs. Still, my legs carried me
forward. I thought of my father, who had been
similarly forced from the palace. I held my head
high and walked under the windows of the king's
apartments, across the marble courtyard, over the
expanse of cobblestone, and out through the gates
of gold.

If the guards turned me out on the streets, I
would suffer from hunger. If I didn't quickly find
some kind of work so that I could buy food, I would
perish. I braced myself against a future as harsh as
the raw wind.

Beyond the gates, several coaches sat. The guards
walked me toward the only coach with a seated
driver, reins ready in his hands. So I wasn't to be
turned out on the streets, at least not here, so close
to Versailles.

The barrel-shaped guard tapped lightly on the
door.

A hand parted the inside curtain slightly, and I heard a woman's voice. "Oui," she said.

The guard let go of my arm, grabbed the golden handle, and opened the door to the coach. He motioned for me to step up, but I hesitated. I trembled, sure that this meant a fate worse than life on the streets. This would be my royal ride to the Bastille, where rats were said to nibble at prisoners in chains. No one would suspect. No one would know. Perhaps even Madame would never learn of my whereabouts or destiny.

"Up with you, now," he said.

In the darkened coach, I fell into an empty velvet seat. When my eyes adjusted to the dim light, I gasped. Across from me, in her usual attire of black from head to foot, sat Madame de Maintenon. I had no idea why she would have anything to do with me. Her presence was the blackest of omens.

"Bonjour, Cécile," she said.

"Bonjour, Madame de Maintenon," I replied, my voice almost escaping me.

"You are no doubt wondering what this all means."

I nodded, hands clasped tightly in my lap.

"The king could not let the defiant behavior of you and Madame de Ventadour and her nursemaids go without punishment. To defy the court doctors brings its consequences. Anjou needs his governess and nurses. You, however, were already suspect. A punishment had to be handed out, and so you . . . your punishment—"

I swallowed again, my throat dry. Was my fate to be death? I began to tremble, trying to comprehend her words.

". . . is banishment from court. Never again are you to return through the gates of Versailles."

I didn't move. My whole future hung on her words.

"I was once like you, Cécile: poor, destitute, and orphaned. I was sent to live with noble relations who gave me only clogs for my feet and the task of caring for their turkeys. I ate shame every day. My options were few. I married a wealthy poet named Scarron, twenty-six years older than I. I was deter- mined to educate myself, to become one of the most

informed women in all of France, and when my
husband died, I was offered the task of caring for a
few of the king's illegitimate children. Eventually,
with great patience, I became close to the king.
Close enough to hold my head high at his side."

I couldn't fathom why Madame de Maintenon
would be telling me about her life. Perhaps she was
trying to make herself feel better before sending
me off to a bleak future. Perhaps her religious
convictions made her feel guilty.

"I still believe in the doctors, but what I see is that
Anjou lives. For whatever part you may have played
in saving him, Cécile, I thank you."

I was stunned, unable to believe what I was hearing.

"Your punishment from the king is banishment,
but because Madame pleaded your case with me—I
was glad to see that high-minded woman beg for
once—I offer you an option outside these gates."

I leaned forward and listened.

Madame had humbled herself to her enemy, on
my behalf? I was deeply moved, fully aware of the
age-old battle between these two women. The last

thing Madame would have wanted was to beg from Madame de Maintenon. I was grateful beyond words.

"Cécile, I see in you a quick mind and a courageous spirit. You have heard of St. Cyr?"

"Oui, Madame," I said.

"It is the first school for girls in all of France. I am a religious woman, and I do what I can for charity. Years ago I decided to do more for girls of nobility whose families had fallen upon hard times. I wanted them to have more options than to be forced into ill-suited marriages or to enter the convent. And so, I started the school."

I hadn't imagined that Madame de Maintenon had a charitable bone in her body. I was wrong.

"The girls are treated well, and learning is encouraged only through kindness, never through harsh beatings, which I strictly forbid."

I had envied Philippe and his chance to study and learn while he worked as a court page. A school for girls, just for the sake of learning . . . this was something I had never imagined for myself. I wanted to pinch myself to be sure that I was awake, that this wasn't just an early-morning dream. Of course, the dream of a perfect life at court had not matched real life. A school for girls would probably not be perfect, either, but it was not a path that dead-ended. Instead, it branched off into the future in many possible directions.

"I took it upon myself to find out more about your family history, Cécile. Usually, a student must have four counts of nobility on the father's side. I have decided to make an exception in your case. Your display of compassion, along with your mother's noble blood, earns you special acceptance at St. Cyr."

I swallowed past the hot ember in my throat. My mother was not the simple peasant woman I had believed her to be. And to my surprise, Madame de Maintenon, dour as she seemed, was not everything I had thought she was, either.

"Well, what do you say to my offer?"

"Oui," I said. "Thank you, Madame de Maintenon. Merci beaucoup."

At that, the old trollop smiled. With her knuckles, she rapped against the coach's roof, and the wheels slowly creaked forward.

I pushed aside the curtain. As we left the grand entrance of the palace, the sun broke across the horizon and glittered off the countless windows of Versailles, where Madame and Philippe and little Anjou would stay. I vowed to write to them as soon as I settled at St. Cyr. I would invite them to come and visit, if that were possible. And perhaps, strange as it seemed, I would begin a correspondence with Madame de Maintenon, to whom I owed this new opportunity. Did I feel grateful to her? I didn't know. Too much had happened for me to feel happy or sad or nearly anything at all. Instead, my life was a tiny boat swept along by a swift current, taking me where it would, and guiding me, I hoped, to safe harbor.

Our coach rolled onto dirt streets, and I glanced back at the palace one last time. The sun's early rays shone on everything below—peasant and king, pigeons and horses—and lit up the damp cobble-stone, turning ordinary dewdrops into diamonds.

The End

Then and Now ♦ *A Girl's Life*

F R A N C E

Within the golden gates of the Versailles palace, everyone lived in the shadow of the "Sun King," as King Louis XIV of France was known. He was one of Europe's most powerful rulers, and the sun was his personal symbol. Like the sun, Louis XIV was the center of his universe, and everything revolved around him. His 72-year reign (1643–1715) was one of the longest in French history, and throughout his reign he lived life on a grand scale. He built the palace of Versailles into one of the largest, most elegant palaces in all of Europe, designed to show his power and wealth. There, in the middle of the French countryside, he surrounded himself with 10,000 servants and *courtiers*, nobles who lived at court to serve him.

Everything about Louis XIV emphasized his power. He wore the biggest and curliest wigs, the rarest jewels, the most delicate lace, and the fanciest shoes in all of France. He

The king's apartments were in the center of the palace, so he could see everything that happened.

favored shoes with high, red heels that showed off the shapeliness of his legs.

Everyone at court followed the latest fashions and dressed to impress, too. Several nights a week, the splendidly dressed courtiers gathered for entertainment. They would hear a concert, watch a play or a ballet, dance, or play cards. During the day, there were hunting parties. The entire court was expected to take

King Louis XIV, seated, with some of his family and the royal governess

part in these activities. The king kept track of his courtiers—and controlled them—by requiring their attendance at all formal events. And at Versailles, *everything* was a formal event—from the king's *lever*, or waking-up ritual, to his going-to-bed routine. The king was never alone, and he was at the center of everything that happened.

The court tailors and seamstresses dressed the court for all these events. In addition to elaborate clothing for the king and courtiers, they made simple, more practical everyday dresses for servants like Cécile. But for a special occasion such as a grand ball, even the servants had new clothes.

Cécile's gown had several layers. Over a linen *chemise*, or underdress, Cécile wore *stays*, a corset-like undergarment made of fabric and whalebone that gave her a stylishly slender figure. Over the stays went a decorated, bell-shaped skirt attached to a low-cut *bodice*, or top, and finally, an outer coat, or *manteau*.

Stays were laced in the back, as tightly as possible.

The manteau was usually in a contrasting color and was made of a heavy satin or velvet, with rich folds ending in a short train. The lace trim of Cécile's chemise showed at the neckline and sleeves. Her shoes, slip-on *mules* with slight heels, echoed the courtiers' fashionable shoes.

This silk mule is embroidered with silver thread.

As a peasant, Cécile could have only dreamed of such a gown. Peasant clothing was simple in design, unadorned, and made of rough, homespun linen or wool. Most peasants wore hand-carved wooden *sabots*, or clogs, which were cheap to make and practical for working in the fields.

In Paris and other French cities, there was a middle class of merchants and tradesmen who lived reasonably comfortable lives. But most of France's people lived in the countryside, farming to try to feed their families. Heavy taxation by the king to pay for his luxurious lifestyle and many wars kept people in poverty. Even during times of famine, like the severe winter of 1709, the king continued to tax his people, and many died of starvation. But in spite of such hardships, peasants often had a better chance of surviving an illness than did members of the royal family, who risked having the life bled out of them by court doctors.

A girl born into a peasant family usually faced a future as the wife of another peasant—a life filled with many children and much hardship. Some people escaped into the church, becoming nuns or priests.

Few peasants knew how to read and write as well as Cécile did. In 1698, schooling for both boys and girls became mandatory in France. Schools were run by the church, and students learned reading, writing,

A French peasant family

arithmetic, and *catechism*, or instruction about the Catholic faith.

St. Cyr was the first boarding
school for girls in France. It offered
an education to poor girls of noble
blood who had few prospects in life
other than marriage or a convent.

Girls in France today have many
more choices than in the past. Free

French schoolgirls today

education is available to everyone, and women can
pursue any career that interests them. French people
travel the world to learn about other cultures, but they
continue to take pride in such French traditions as
trendsetting fashion and fine food. Although France no
longer has a king or queen, Versailles remains one of the
most beautiful and most visited palaces in all of Europe.

Today, it is mainly tourists who pass through Versailles's gates of gold.

Glossary of French Words

allez (*ah-lay*)—go

Anjou (*ahn-zhoo*)—a region of France of which one of the king's great-grandsons was the duke

au secours (*oh seh-koor*)—help

Bastille (*bah-steel*)—France's main prison

bonjour (*bohn-zhoor*)—hello

bonsoir (*bohn-swahr*)—good evening

Bourgogne (*boor-guhn-yeh*)—Burgundy, a region of France of which the king's grandson was the duke

Bretagne (*breh-tahn-yeh*)—Brittany, a region of France of which one of the king's great-grandsons was the duke

Cendrillon (*sahn-dree-yohn*)—Cinderella

chaise longue (*shehz long*)—an upholstered reclining chair

chemise (*shuh-meez*)—a lightweight shift, or undergarment

chéri (*shay-ree*)—an endearment, such as "dear one"

dauphin (*doh-fehn*)—the prince who is in line to become the next king

dauphine (*doh-feen*)—the wife of a dauphin

de (*deh*)—of

duc, duchesse (*dook*, *duh-shess*)—duke, duchess

Fontainebleau (*fohn-tahn-bloh*)—one of the king's royal palaces

gouttes d'Angleterre (*goot dahn-gluh-tahr*)—English drops, a common medicine of the 1700s

la, le (*lah*, *luh*)—the (feminine, masculine)

lever (*leh-vay*)—the king's morning rising ritual

Madame (*mah-dahm*)—Mrs. or madam

Mademoiselle (*mahd-mwah-zel*)—Miss

Maman (*mah-mahn*)—Mother

manteau (*mahn-toh*)—coat

Ménagerie (*may-nah-zher-ee*)—a collection of wild or exotic animals, as in a small zoo

merci beaucoup (*mehr-see bo-coo*)—thank you very much

Mon Dieu! (*mohn dyuh*)—my God!, or good heavens!

Monsieur (*muh-syer*)—Mr. or sir

Noailles (*noh-eyeh*)—a region of France

non (*nohn*)—no

Orangerie (*oh-rahn-zher-ee*)—orange grove

oui (*wee*)—yes

Rileaux (*ree-loh*)—the name of Cécile's village

sabots (*sah-boh*)—wooden clogs

s'il vous plaît (*see voo play*)—please

St. Cyr (*san seer*)—the boarding school for girls of
noble families founded by Madame de Maintenon

toilette (*twah-let*)—washing up, brushing one's hair,
and dressing to prepare for the day

très bien (*tray byen*)—very good

Versailles (*vehr-sigh*)—the French town where King
Louis XIV's main palace was located; also the
name of the palace

Author's Note

Though the story of Cécile is a work of fiction,
the setting of Versailles and the major events of
this time period are true. From my imagination,
I created Cécile, her parents, Philippe, Françoise,
and a few nameless servants and guards. All the
other characters are taken from history and express
the roles they played at court during the story's time.

For research, I traveled to France and spent a
week at Versailles, where I roamed the palace,
walked and biked over the vast grounds, and floated
on the Grand Canal. As with every book I write, I
tried to absorb the story's setting with my five senses.
When I returned home, I pored over stacks of history
books, hoping to write a story as true as possible.

Madame did write many letters, which give
readers a personal glimpse into the daily lives of
people at the French court. Her letters are gathered
and translated in a book called *A Woman's Life in the
Court of the Sun King*. Writing was a way for her to
cope with what was often a lonely existence at court,

and indeed, her dogs were her closest companions. It is true, Madame loved to hunt, and she claimed to have survived twenty-seven falls from horseback.

Louis XIV lived to age seventy-seven, despite the doctors' barbaric medical procedures. He never got over the deaths of Marie-Adélaïde, the Duc de Bourgogne (his grandson), and Bretagne (his great-grandson). As the king aged, he saw all hardship and tragedy as God's punishment upon him for his pride and arrogance. He regretted having spent so much of his life building his empire and warring with neighboring countries. Madame de Maintenon stayed at his side until he died, after which she left the palace to live at St. Cyr, her brainchild and the first boarding school for girls in France.

Anjou survived measles, thanks to his brave governess, Madame de Ventadour, and her nursemaids, who heroically barricaded themselves in a room with the feverish child, refusing to allow the doctors to treat him. He grew up to become King Louis XV, a man who loved to make clocks more than make war.

Mary Casanova

800L